I0570409

Novels by Kelly Cheek

All We Hold Dear

Trial by Fire

The Lost Colony

JackSimile and the Phantom Fury

Spirit Breather

The SpiritSense Trilogy

In Restless Dreams

First Light

When We Were Gone Astray

The Facebook Trilogy

Profile

Private Messages

Poked

FIRST LIGHT

Kelly Cheek

Cover and book design by Kelly Cheek

ISBN: 978-1-7335022-5-2

Printed in the United States of America

The real meaning of enlightenment is to gaze with undimmed eyes on all darkness.

Nikos Kazantzakis

People only see what they are prepared to see.

Ralph Waldo Emerson

1

Fin MacKinley stared at the page on his computer, willing an idea to show itself. The great mass of white was inviting, a blank page full of opportunity, just waiting for a sentence, a word, a letter to be placed upon it. To Fin, it was intimidating, taunting him. Despite his attempts at brute force mentalism, the ideas remained elusive.

The perils of a perfectionist prose-ologist.

However, the problem wasn't a lack of words, but a lack of ideas. He fondly remembered back when he was young, when the ideas flowed like hormones. But he was only writing short stories back then, and mediocre ones at that, not full-length novels. And he was just a teenager. He remembered that his character-development had left a little to be desired.

Still . . .

Fin's big break came just a few years ago. Having been a self-published author for a while, he had forced himself to be content with a few scattered sales through Amazon when somebody stumbled across one of his books. But when one of the big guys in New York discovered *TimePlex* and asked to publish it on the mass market, Fin jumped at the opportunity. When somebody subsequently bought the movie rights and produced a major motion picture, starring Ryan Reynolds and Jennifer Lawrence no less, Fin knew he had 'made it.'

A Place Made of Time, the sequel to *TimePlex,* had given him a little trouble as well. But after an exceedingly eventful trip to Scotland, the setting of the story, he had been inspired to finish it, to his agent's delight. The movie rights for the sequel had also been purchased, but as of now, it was only in early pre-production.

Still, his agent was anxious for news about a follow-up to his previous successes.

Fin was, too.

He didn't remember having this much trouble before he became a 'traditionally-published' author. Sure, he had the occasional blocks that he had to struggle through, but the ideas were always there. It was just a matter of figuring out how to present them.

Now, there was always the pressure of having a deadline for squeezing out the next one.

This damn headache wasn't helping. He had never been plagued with migraines before, but from what he'd heard about them, it seemed as if he was starting.

It also didn't help that he was distracted by Suzy's upcoming visit. He had met Suzy Quinn through the genealogy site they both used, and had, last summer, taken a trip to Scotland with her. Her unique recently-discovered talents of communicating with ghosts proved particularly well-suited to extricating them from a sticky situation which, admittedly, she had been responsible for getting them into. All in all, though, it had made for an interesting finale to their vacation.

The romance that had developed between them, however, was left in a less-than-satisfying condition. Mourning the death of her husband and daughter nearly two years before, she had determined that she wasn't ready to seriously pursue a relationship.

So she stayed there in Marblehead, Massachusetts, in her family estate, while Fin came back to his home southwest of Denver, Colorado. He lived in one of those neighborhoods on the cusp between suburbia and wilderness. A few years back, a developer, seeing dollar signs, started building houses up the side of the foothills. Fortunately, for Fin at least, the developer ran out of money or buyers. Fin's house was the last one before the winding road ended at a small, remote trailhead into the woods.

Fin pulled his attention back to the blank page on his computer and sighed. He immediately felt bad about his silent complaints. A few months ago, he had mentioned his occasional difficulty with writer's block to Suzy, and complained about how frustrating it was.

"My husband and daughter died because of me," she replied in a flat, matter-of-fact tone.

From that moment, Fin realized that his little intermittent bouts of writer's block were not that big. He just had to deal with it.

The nightmares, though, they were a little tougher to handle. He closed his eyes at night and he would hear the darkness whispering hoarsely at him, usually in a Scottish accent. Ever since their experience in the Edinburgh vaults, and subsequently in Suzy's carriage house, those evil faces periodically appeared in his dreams. But even that was becoming less frequent, so he dealt with it.

As his mind was in 'reliving the past mode,' he remembered the appearance he made at Comic Con New York, before *TimePlex,* the movie, premiered. Appearing on stage with Ryan Reynolds and Jennifer Lawrence, the stars of the movie, and Janek Laar, the director, had been quite a humbling experience.

But during the interview, he had mentioned Suzy's experience with the ghost in her carriage house, and Janek had said, "Maybe a joint ghost story is in our future." Fin hadn't given any thought to that statement at the time. But maybe there was something to it. His experience with Suzy in the vaults and in her carriage house were certainly of the 'stranger than fiction' variety. Maybe there really was a story in there.

§

After a day of pondering, Fin was beginning to like the idea of writing a ghost story. He didn't actually have a story yet, but that would come. Basic ideas and settings usually appeared first. After deliberating on it a while, the story would usually develop in his mind.

He thought about it as he fell asleep, if he woke up to turn over or go to the bathroom during the night, and when he woke in the morning. Once an idea presented itself, it would stubbornly stay in his head whenever his mind wasn't actively involved in something else, until he was able to start developing it into a usable story.

So during the one-and-a-half-hour drive from his house southwest of Denver to the airport northeast of Denver, the story idea was on his mind.

That, and Suzy.

As he got closer to the terminal, though, he had to focus on where he was going. According to the signs, the United Airlines gates were located in the West Terminal, so he followed the directions to passenger pickup on the west side, under the big white 'tent' that covered the airport.

Once he was under the structure, he watched the succession of signs for United, and started scanning the arriving passengers. Then, he saw her.

She saw his red Tesla about the same time he saw her, and she waved. Fin pulled into an open space by the curb and quickly got out. Since Denver International Airport was the largest airport in North America, and one of the busiest, they didn't have time for much of a greeting, but they couldn't help going in for a quick hug before Fin picked up Suzy's suitcase and stuck it in his trunk.

Emerging from the structure and back into the sunlight, Fin looked over at Suzy, squinting from the sudden light.

"Hi," he said with a goofy smile.

"Hi yourself," she smiled back at him. Fin remembered the somewhat aloof smartass persona she usually projected, and he felt a warm feeling in his chest when he saw the sweet smile she gave him now.

"God, it's good to see you!" Fin said.

"You're going to get all mushy now, aren't you?"

"There it is," Fin replied.

"What?"

"I thought you might have left your snark back at home in Marblehead."

"Psh," she scoffed. "I never leave home without it." Suddenly, she was distracted as she looked ahead of them. "Oh my god! What the hell is that?"

Fin looked in the direction she was looking.

"Ah, that's Blucifer." Outside the airport, the giant blue horse sculpture with the glowing red eyes drew mixed reactions from both locals and visitors. "He actually killed his creator."

"Bullshit."

"No, really. The horse's head fell on the artist in his studio in New Mexico while he was still working on it. He died there."

"I wonder if he's still there," Suzy said quietly. Fin knew what she meant and stole a quick glance at her.

"How was your flight?" he asked, hoping to steer the conversation in a more cheerful direction.

"It was fine. Uneventful, just the way I like them."

"Good."

"So, what's on the agenda?" Suzy asked, rubbing her hands together.

"Lotsa lovin'," Fin said, forcing a hick, country accent. "Maybe some eatin'."

"Okay, and in between these episodes of sexual and gastronomical gratification?"

"Resting, obviously!" He smiled, then went on to give a serious response. "I have one reservation already made, but I'm wondering about something else." Suzy turned her attention to him, curious. "What do you think about going to the Stanley Hotel up in Estes Park? It's where Stephen King stayed several years ago, and where he was inspired to write *The Shining*."

"It's haunted?" Suzy asked.

"Supposedly. I took one of their ghost tours with my ex a few years ago, and I didn't witness any evidence. Neither did anybody else in our group, but there have been others who swear to it. Parts of *Dumb and Dumber* were filmed there, and after just three hours in room 217, Stephen King's room, Jim Carrey ran out of there demanding to stay someplace else. He would only return there to film his scenes at the last second, and then rush back out."

"And what makes you think I'd want to go there?" Suzy asked.

"Well," Fin started hesitantly, "I just thought you might want to, you know, set the spirits free, let them know they can move on."

"And become one of the most hated people in America?"

"Huh?"

"People love their ghost stories. I mean sure, there are some that are malevolent and harmful, and if they're hurting others in some way, they *should* go. But for the most part, a lot of these are just beloved, albeit scary, legends."

"But . . . okay, I'm confused. You sent those ghosts away in the vaults, and in your carriage house."

"Because they were hurting others. The ones in the vaults kept the Caspers terrified." After their episode there in the Edinburgh vaults, they had begun referring to the friendly ghosts as Caspers. "You remember how terrified little Catriona was."

"I do," Fin replied, nodding.

"And your foul forebear was keeping my admirable ancestor a virtual prisoner."

"Nice alliteration," Fin smiled.

"Thank you. So just think about how despised I would become if I ran off those Caspers from people's lives. And the lawsuits! I imagine the Stanley Hotel makes a lot of money off their ghostly reputation."

"Yeah, I suppose so."

"I mean," Suzy continued, "I guess the argument could be made that the ghosts' well-being should be considered, too. But again, if they're not harming others, well, I just don't have the energy or the inclination to be expelling ghosts everywhere I go. Despite Lilith's belief in me." Lilith was an acquaintance that Suzy had consulted on a few occasions. She was an expert on ghosts, or 'spirits' as she preferred, who lived in Marblehead, near Suzy.

"What belief is that?"

"That I'm a lightworker."

"What's a lightworker?"

"It's a new age term," Suzy replied with a sigh. "It's someone who was placed on earth for some kind of higher purpose, usually having to do with bettering the lives of others. Somebody with what Lilith calls SpiritSense. I forget all the various criteria, but they're supposed to be highly intuitive and connect with people on something of a psychic level, to improve their lot in life. Or death, in my case."

"Yeah, that doesn't sound like you at all," Fin teased.

"At any rate," Suzy replied seriously, "I don't think I have it in me to go around sending ghosts on to the next plane everywhere I go."

"Okay," Fin said. "That makes sense."

"So, this reservation you made?" Suzy said, happy to change the subject.

"I rented us a nice little B&B in Silver Plume, an old silver mining town up in the mountains. It's a beautiful setting, and I thought a few days there would be a nice introduction to someone who hasn't visited Colorado before."

"Sounds wonderful!" Suzy replied, as she leaned back in her seat and slipped her hand into Fin's.

2

Suzy woke up to sunlight streaming through the clerestory window set high in the eave of the cathedral ceiling in Fin's bedroom. She stretched luxuriantly, careful to not make any noise, as she marveled at the blueness of the April sky through the window.

She turned and looked at Fin, snoring softly beside her. She spent a fond moment or two remembering the night before. Fin's lovemaking was the perfect mixture of gentle and ardent, sensitive and passionate. She had never known a man so responsive to her needs.

She sat up against the headboard, moving slowly so as to not wake Fin, and she looked around the room. She hadn't really looked it over much the night before. Her attention had been elsewhere. There were only a few pictures on the walls. Over the bed was a collection of prints of sensuous-looking women in natural settings, by a nineteenth-century artist named Alphonse Mucha, whom Fin said was his favorite.

The walls on either side were bare. But across the room, next to the French doors onto his balcony, was an arrangement of pictures, family photographs. In the center was an 8 x 10 color photograph of Fin, his parents and sister in what looked like one of those posed Sears family photo portraits. Around that were smaller candid photos of his parents and his sister, separately and together. They looked like a happy family.

She knew there was more to the story, though. She remembered him telling her about them last year during a romantic walk on the shore of Loch Ness when they were visiting Scotland. His family lived in Kansas, just a few hours' drive away, but they didn't have much contact with him due to their staunch religious beliefs conflicting with his writing stories that contained an occasional explicit or 'immoral' scene.

"You know, it's funny," Fin said beside her, "I thought your eyes were blue."

"They are," Suzy said, turning to see him staring at her nipples. Making a scoffing sound, she pulled the sheet up over her breasts.

"Oh yeah, there they are," he said, looking up at her face. He put his arm around her waist and pulled her back down beside him. "Good morning."

"Morning, smartass," Suzy smiled, kissing him. She looked at him for a few moments. "I was just looking at the pictures of your family over there. Have you seen or spoken to them recently?"

Fin made a face and didn't answer immediately.

"No," he finally said. "A couple of months ago, I told them about my experiences involving the ghosts, at your place and in Scotland. They pretty much made the shunning official at that point."

"What? Why?"

"Well, I told you they were religious. From that standpoint, they thought those experiences were just proof that I was lost. 'Toying with the devil,' was the phrase they used."

"Oh my god," Suzy said indignantly, "what a shitty thing to do!"

"Yeah, well, I can understand it."

"You can?" Her tone expressed disbelief.

"Sure. Everybody has a certain belief system, some platform that serves as the foundation of their faith, whether that faith is sacred or secular. My family's doctrine is based on their church's interpretation of scriptures that they believe and embrace completely."

"Yes, but you're family."

"They feel that they're part of God's family, and what he says goes. He outranks me. He's the head of the spiritual family, so their interpretation of his wishes overshadows physical family ties. It sucks, but like I said, I understand it."

Suzy put her arms around him and held him tightly.

"You're obviously a lot more forgiving than I am," she said in a sympathetic tone, feeling righteous indignation for him.

"Well, something I've learned over the years is that forgiveness does more for the giver than the receiver."

"Ah, so forgiving them is purely an act of selfishness?" Suzy smiled a smartass smile.

"More like self-preservation."

§

Fin made French toast and sausage for breakfast, and as he worked, Suzy perched on a stool at his kitchen counter. For a while, he was focused on what he was doing, and unaware that Suzy was quietly watching him. His posture was relaxed and comfortable, and Suzy tilted her head a little as she studied him. She felt something, a warm little tingle in her gut, which she hadn't felt in quite some time.

As she was watching him, Fin happened to glance over at her and stopped, suddenly self-conscious.

"What?" he asked.

Suzy smiled and shook her head.

"I just don't think I've ever seen a man so at home in the kitchen," she said.

Fin wiggled an eyebrow and managed a fairly deft twirl of the spatula.

"I did most of the cooking when I was married to Kay," he smiled.

"Are you sure I can't do anything to help?"

"Nope, just watch and be amazed."

"Okay, so talk to me."

"Talk to you?" Fin said, looking expectantly at her. "I'm an introvert. I'm going to need a little more of a prompt than that."

"Okay, tell me about your life before I came along."

"Ah, the dark times," Fin said in an ominous voice, but he smiled to counterbalance it.

"Why was it dark?"

"It wasn't all dark, by any means. It was quite dark after Kay left me, though. I never had many friends, and those I did have were mostly Kay's friends. So after that, I was pretty much alone."

"Didn't you tell me that *TimePlex* was discovered and published just a few weeks after the two of you split up?" Suzy asked.

"That's true, but fame and fortune don't make a life. And besides it took almost a year before my book actually started selling and hit the *New York Times* bestseller list. And got the attention of Hollywood.

"So until I started seeing any results from my literary toils, I kept up my daily grind. I'd get up and go to work, do my shift, then go home and decompress. Read or watch TV or something like that."

"You were in construction, right?" Suzy asked, noting the slender lines of his body, visually tracing the V from his shoulders to his narrow waist.

"Yes, and I hated it," he said as he lifted the latest slices of French toast from the skillet and placed them on a platter warming in the oven. "At least I wasn't working for Kay's father anymore, but still, I had to support myself. So I'd get up the next morning and do it all again. Weekends weren't much different, except for the job."

"But, what about the guys you worked with? Weren't they friends?"

"Not really," he replied, battering the next slice and placing it in the sizzling pan. "I wasn't like them. They were extroverts and drinkers and sports fiends. I did go out for a beer with them after work a couple of times, but I never really felt comfortable in their company. So I spent my free time alone. Usually writing or browsing Facebook or watching TV.

"I usually didn't even bother to open the blinds. So, in that sense, they *were* dark times. I'd just sit there in my dim little apartment all alone and depressed.

"Yes, I was feeling sorry for myself," he said, looking defiantly at Suzy. "Don't judge me." Suzy shook her head and smiled.

"Once in a while, I'd realize that I wasn't going to make new friends by staying by myself in my apartment. So I'd get myself cleaned up and dressed and go out to one of the popular hangouts in the area.

"And then I'd sit there and eat and drink all alone. I was still shy. That's when I realized how much I had relied on my marriage. Whenever Kay and I were with other people, I was usually with her. She served as the buffer between me and them. Now, without that buffer, I didn't know what to say. I could respond to direct questions, sometimes even cleverly, but trying to *initiate* a conversation would leave me wobbly or tongue-tied."

"Which is why you needed a prompt now," Suzy said.

"Exactly," Fin replied, punctuating his response with the spatula. He leaned casually against the stove as he continued, and Suzy tried to concentrate on what he was saying instead of focusing on his long fingers as he nimbly flipped the French toast. "So, feeling discouraged, I'd finish my lonely dinner and drink, pay the bill, and retreat back into my comfortable little hermit life until I felt the need to venture out again."

"But," Suzy interjected, "I thought you *preferred* being alone."

"Sometimes, but not always. I'm naturally an introvert. I'm *not* naturally a hermit. Introverts still get lonely."

"Okay, I'm on the introversion scale myself, so I understand that."

"So, after a few weeks of repeating that tiresome cycle, I finally remembered a recommendation a coworker had given me after Kay left, about a particular dating site. I missed hanging out with other people occasionally, but I also missed feminine companionship. I missed having a soft little thing there to caress me and say 'poor baby' if I had a bad day. Of course, it's not like I had that when I was married to Kay. I missed it then, too.

"So anyway, I got my laptop, opened up the browser and in the URL window, I typed 'MySoulmate.com.'" He screwed up his face a little at the hokey sound of it, then rolled the sausage links in the pan. "I remember hesitating.

"Was I really about to jump into a dating site?" He turned his attention away from the skillet for a moment to look sideways at Suzy with what she thought of as a 'little boy' expression. "I felt weak and feeble in the face of my shyness and making new friends, let alone meeting women. So, maybe getting help in this facet of my life would help me to build confidence, and maybe even find a measure of happiness.

"At least that was my reasoning." He turned back to the skillet and turned a slice. "Anyway, realizing my desperation, I hit 'Enter.' I watched for a moment as a predominantly blue page scattered with lots of photographs of beautiful women and handsome men opened up on my screen.

"I was encouraged by that. As I was about to embark on this expedition of shopping for a woman, it was nice to see the kind of selection there was to choose from. Although the good-looking men were a little intimidating. I was up against some stiff competition."

"You do realize they were probably just models, right?" Suzy asked.

"Yes, I did. Shut up. This is *my* story." Suzy grinned and closed her mouth.

"There was a button that said, 'Find Your Soulmate.' I clicked it, and a new page opened where I had to start creating my own profile, starting with a username.

"I started thinking along the lines of construction, and names like 'ErectionMan' began coming to mind. I'm a guy, that's what we do." Suzy smirked. "But then, I thought that, since I didn't enjoy my job in construction, why should I draw attention to it?

"I won't relate my entire thought process. What I settled on was the fact that I'm six feet tall, and I live in the Mile High City. My username became 'AltiDood.' I selected a password and moved on to the next page.

"Here, I was asked for at least one picture for my profile. I hadn't really thought that far ahead, but after making sure that my hair was in place and that I didn't have anything stuck between my teeth, I snapped a couple of pictures with the webcam built into my laptop."

"Oh, I hate those," Suzy said. "I always look like such a dork in those pictures."

Fin shrugged and turned up one corner of his mouth in response.

"It's not so bad if you make sure you have the angle right. And don't look at the screen. Look at the lens."

Suzy wasn't entirely convinced.

"Anyway, from there, I was asked to write a little about myself. That was a little more comfortable for me, being a writer. Although writing about *myself,* talking myself up, telling what a great catch I am, that was a little harder. Fortunately, there were some prompts. 'What do you like to do in your free time?' 'What are your favorite foods?' 'What are you looking for in a soulmate?' That sort of thing.

"I managed to sound like a reasonably decent guy. I didn't have much, I was usually broke, and I was bitter about Kay, but still, I was relatively unspoiled. And I was still naïve enough to believe that there was somebody out there for me, though I admit that I kind of had my doubts about anything as deep as a 'soulmate.' In fact, I wasn't even sure such a thing existed, though I was still hopeful."

"I can see that," Suzy said warmly. "Your hopefulness. I know I give you shit about it sometimes," she admitted, "but I do admire that in this cynical age, that you haven't given up on me yet."

"A hopeful romantic," Fin replied, focusing on continuing his thought, and trying not to get sidetracked by Suzy's encouraging admission. "That's what I called myself." Suzy smiled, her admiration clearly showing in her eyes.

"But after spending a little time with the setup and polishing of my profile, I was finally able to get down to the business of shopping for a woman."

"So, women are just a consumer commodity, huh?" Lest she sound too combative, she grinned flirtatiously. Fin flashed a crooked smile at her, knowing his tease had hit home.

"The site gave me a page with several photographs of potential soulmates, all within about five to ten miles of where I lived. The next step was to pick out the ones I liked and make contact."

"God, that sounds grueling. I don't think I could do it."

"Initially, I was a little overeager," Fin shrugged, "and didn't really think it through very well. The first couple of introductory e-mails I sent were pretty bad. 'Hey, I like your profile. Wanna meet?'" Suzy smirked at that.

"I discovered that the anonymity of online communication did help to mask my shyness, though. In fact, I was surprised by how easy it was for me to actually 'approach' a woman I'd never met before, hiding behind my online persona, and ask her out."

"Yeah," Suzy said, "you seemed very comfortable in our initial exchanges through the genealogy site."

"That was just unheard of for me before that, in real life. After a while, I went back and read through some of the messages I wrote, and I was amazed at how confident and witty I seemed." He looked at Suzy with that half smile that she loved. But she didn't want to tell him that. "It helped that I was able to take my time to say the right thing, rather than just mumbling around whichever foot I had stuffed in my mouth, as I often did in face-to-face conversation."

"So, did you have any success?" Suzy asked.

"Not as much as I had on our genealogy site." Fin smiled at her, then turned back to the skillet and placed the last piece of French toast on the platter, turning off the stove. He picked up the platter and turned toward Suzy, and was surprised by the warmth of the smile she was bathing him in.

§

From the eastern United States, I-70 cuts a relatively smooth continuous swath across the country. Once it gets into Colorado, though, it becomes much more jagged as it zigs and zags its way through the Precambrian tectonic disturbance, known as the Rocky Mountains, that divides the state.

Under the beautiful blue sky that Suzy woke up to, Fin drove west into the mountains on I-70.

"You had me jabbering quite a bit earlier this morning before breakfast," Fin said. "It's your turn. Talk to me. Have you sent any more ghosts into the great beyond since we were together?"

"No," Suzy replied wistfully. Fin thought she sounded sad. He glanced at her.

"You sound unhappy about that."

Suzy squinted for a moment, pondering.

"No, not unhappy. I just miss Fiona. I got pretty close to her in the few months that we were together."

"Of course. You basically lived her life for a while. Whatever happened with her baby?"

"Not much," Suzy replied and turned to look out her window. Fin got the impression she was hiding tears.

"Honey, what's wrong?" he asked. Suzy sighed and wiped her eyes.

"It's silly," she said. "It's not even my baby."

"It's not silly," Fin countered, putting his hand on her knee. "Like I said, you were seeing Fiona's life from her point of view. I remember you told me that you felt what she felt, so I think it's only natural that you would have strong feelings about her dead baby. Not to mention the empathy factor, having lost your own daughter."

Suzy sniffed, and she put her hand on Fin's.

"He's still packed in the plastic bin Jay put him in a year and a half ago."

"Did you tell him what you know about the baby?"

"I did," she scoffed. "After the article in that Salem rag, and then the riot at my place, pretty much everybody knew what was going on with me anyway, so I figured I might as well fill him in. But second-hand information passed down from a ghost doesn't qualify as provenance, especially when Jay doesn't believe in ghosts.

"So when somebody comes to the museum and donates anything from a rusty fish hook to a yellowed handkerchief, it seems to take precedence over the mummified baby of my ghostly ancestress."

"I know I'm speaking from an introvert's point of view," Fin pondered, "but I'm not sure which would be better, being filed away in a plastic bin, or being on display for the world to see like a freak of nature."

"Being acknowledged would be better, for the baby *and* for Fiona," Suzy replied a little more fiercely than she intended. She looked at Fin with a contrite expression, and she sighed again. "I'm sorry. It's just that I'm beginning to understand what being a freak of nature feels like. Everybody who knows me now knows that I'm the crazy lady who talks to ghosts."

Fin squeezed her knee affectionately, then put his hand back on the wheel. Working their way westward into the mountains, the twists and turns in the road required more control.

"I guess it's a good thing I'm closer to the introvert end of the scale myself," Suzy continued. "Being with most people now is a pain in the ass."

"Maybe you just need some new friends."

"Hmm, that may be," Suzy agreed, feeling a little surprised at the revelation. "I mean seriously, you and Rachel, and maybe a couple of others, are the only ones I can tolerate for more than an hour or two."

"A ringing endorsement if I ever heard one!" Fin grinned. "I know what you mean, though. I don't have a lot in common with some of the folks I know. After *TimePlex* was published, while I was still working my construction job, I took a few copies to work with me, in case anybody wanted to get one. A couple of them were very complimentary. 'It's really thick!' one of them said."

"Thick?" Suzy snickered.

"They couldn't imagine stringing that many sentences together into a coherent story that made a book of such substantial dimensions. I guess acknowledging its ponderous proportions was the best compliment he could think of."

"Did they buy any copies?"

"No," Fin replied, shaking his head.

They passed a few curves in silence before Fin spoke again. "You want to know something that I've just realized? Being an introvert, I need time alone after spending time with other people. Except with you. You're the only person I know who doesn't greatly extend my necessary recharge time. In fact, if anything, you accelerate it. I feel energized whenever I'm with you."

Suzy looked at him for a moment, her eyes narrowed a bit, her face introspective.

"My first inclination was to make a smartass comment about you getting all mushy. But I realized that I feel the same way. You're easy to be with." Fin glanced at her with a smile. "You're even-tempered and laid-back. You don't get all pushed out of shape about something I've said, even if it *was* a smartass remark."

"We're MFEO, babe," Fin replied.

"Huh?" Suzy asked, her face scrunched up.

"It's from *Sleepless in Seattle*. MFEO means we're made for each other."

"Ah," Suzy said ambiguously.

They drove the next few miles in silence, immersed in their own thoughts, until Fin's GPS instructed him to take

Exit 226. Once they came down off the highway, they turned into the little town of Silver Plume.

"Wow," Suzy commented, "these streets are about as narrow as some of Marblehead's streets. And unpaved. Even Main Street is a gravel road." Fin nodded as he followed the directions of the GPS.

Unlike Marblehead, the streets followed something of a grid pattern, despite the scattered outcroppings of granite that rose out of the ground. These formed the irregular northern perimeter of the town, eventually rising to become Silver Plume Mountain, 12,428 feet high at its peak.

After only a minute or so of driving through the little town, they pulled up in front of a charming house with gingerbread trim at the base of the mountain, nestled behind several aspen and fir trees. A carved and painted wooden sign said "Mountain Melody" emblazoned over a pair of capital Ms in a nineteenth-century style. Fin and Suzy got out of the car and stretched, walking up toward the house.

A grizzled old man sitting in a rocking chair on the front porch looked up at them as they approached. He pushed himself up out of the chair and stood in a nearly upright position, in old overalls that were some indistinguishable color between blue and brown. He looked almost as if he might have been around since the silver rush. He pushed his white hair back with his gnarled hands and smoothed his beard as they stepped up on the porch.

"You checkin' in?" he asked in a friendly but abrupt manner.

"Yes," Fin replied.

"Come on in. I'll get my daughter. She runs this place."

He opened the screen door and held it open, leading them inside. As the old man went down a hall toward the back of the house, Fin and Suzy stayed near the door and looked around.

To their left was a sitting room decorated in an eclectic mix of rustic old west and mining paraphernalia and classic

Victorian décor. A stone fireplace, darkened from many fires, was the focal point of the room, with a collection of comfortable-looking furniture arranged around it, and several shelves filled with games and books. Fin could see some novels mixed with an abundance of books dealing with mining, local biographies and the history of the area. Opposite the fireplace was an antique upright piano with stacks of song books and sheet music.

To the right was a dining room. Two tables, each with six chairs of about five different but somewhat similar styles stood in the sunny and inviting room, cleared now from the morning's repast.

They looked up as they heard footsteps from the back of the house, and a robust sixty-something woman wearing thick glasses approached them with a smile. Her father followed behind her more slowly.

"Welcome," she said. "Are you Fin?"

"I am," Fin replied, shaking her outstretched hand. "And this is Suzy."

"Hi, Suzy," she said warmly, extending her hand and her smile. "I'm Dolores Watkins. And you met my father, Jim?" Her father nodded and smiled a semi-toothless grin as he shuffled past, back out to the front porch. Fin couldn't help thinking of Stinky Pete, the prospector character from *Toy Story* 2.

"Yes," Fin said. "Sorry if we're a little early. I guess I forgot it's only an hour drive up here."

"Not a problem at all," Dolores said, waving it off. "I just finished getting it ready for you." She put a sheet of paper down on a table that stood in the entryway with a tin cup of ballpoint pens. "I'll just have you sign this and I'll show you to your room."

It was a standard check-in sheet that could have been from any modern hotel. He glanced at the information on the sheet and, seeing that everything was correct, signed his name.

"Wonderful," Dolores said, smiling as she picked up the paper. She looked it over to be sure everything was taken care of. "And you've already paid for your stay, so there's nothing more I need from you."

She folded the paper in half and stuck it in a large pocket on the front of her apron. Fin dropped the pen back in the tin cup.

"Follow me," she said as she turned back down the hallway.

"This is a lovely place," Suzy said as they followed her lead. "Do you live here yourself?"

"Thank you," Dolores said. "Yes, my father and I live at the back of the house. It's a labor of love. My great-grandmother started this place as a boarding house. I've been here my whole life. This way."

She turned up a steep staircase, and Fin and Suzy followed her. At the top of the stairs, she stopped at one of the doors in the oddly-shaped hall, distorted by the shape of the converging gables. She slipped a key into the lock and opened the door.

The room was welcoming, and was decorated in a garden theme, with pictures of mountain wildflowers in frames made from what looked like old distressed fence pickets. There was an old-fashioned bed and a small table with two upholstered chairs.

Against the wall opposite the bed was a washstand with a pitcher and bowl, and arranged in the pitcher were a dozen red roses. Next to it was an antique silver ice bucket standing on an embroidered towel, condensation just beginning to form on it. There was a bottle of champagne cooling in it.

"Here are your keys," Dolores said, handing them to Fin. "Breakfast is between seven and nine. If there's anything you need, please don't hesitate to ask. Happy birthday, Suzy," she smiled, as she stepped out of the door and closed it behind her.

"Happy birthday?" Suzy asked, her face displaying surprise.

"I know I'm a few days late," Fin said, "but you weren't here on your birthday."

"How did you know my birthday?"

"You're forgetting our lives are connected by our distant ancestors. Your birthday is on your personal data page at FamilyLine.com."

Suzy's eyes blurred with tears as she looked back at the roses. She bent over to smell them, and Fin was beside her when she straightened back up.

"Happy birthday, sweetheart," he said.

"Dammit, Fin," she said, "I didn't want to get all mushy this early in my visit." As if she couldn't resist the pull, she turned into his waiting arms, her body conforming to his to fit as tightly against him as possible. They stayed like that for a couple of minutes, not speaking, just holding each other, basking in the closeness, feeling the rhythm of their breathing against each other.

As time passed and they felt the continued closeness, their hands began moving, caressing, exploring. The sweetness gradually turned into heat, and Suzy put her head back. Fin moved his left hand up to cradle the back of her head as he kissed her. His right hand moved down her back and over the soft twin curves of her butt, and he grabbed a handful.

Eventually, it seemed to Fin that Suzy was even more eager than he was, if that was even possible. Her hands were inside his shirt, kneading his back, her fingertips digging into him. She pulled him close, her breasts pressing deliciously against his chest.

Slipping his hand up Suzy's blouse, Fin caressed her back for a few moments, before centering in on her bra. Gripping the end, he pulled the hooks loose and felt the sweet release of pressure as her bra unfastened and her breasts softened against his chest.

The mutual oral exploration they were both engaged in continued for a few moments until Suzy pulled away from him. Panting, her breasts rising and falling with each tantalizing breath, she quickly tugged at the buttons and whipped her blouse off.

In a time that rivaled her own, Fin had his own shirt off, and they came back together for another kiss, more aroused now by the skin-to-skin contact. With their passion rising, they both reluctantly separated for two and a half seconds to rip off their jeans. About 1.9 seconds after that, they had the covers pulled down and were happily coupled in the fresh, cool sheets.

§

The ice in the ice bucket was mostly melted by the time Fin got up, but the champagne was refreshingly cold. They sat in bed talking, caressing each other, drinking champagne, until the rays of sunlight shining between the slats of the wooden blinds were coming in at a much more oblique angle.

Finding that there were no restaurants in Silver Plume, other than a coffee shop open only on the weekend, they drove five miles back to Georgetown for dinner. They spent a quiet evening in private exploration of their deepening feelings.

3

The valley was blanketed with colorful wildflowers which swayed in the gentle mountain breeze. Walls of stone rose on each side of the valley, framing the scene in Suzy's view.

"How beautiful!" she thought as she appreciated the rainbow of colors. As she watched, though, they started doing something she had never seen flowers do. They began moving independently from the breeze, coalescing into patches of similar colors. Golden asters came together to create patches of yellow, milkvetch and bell flowers congregated into shades of blue, fairy trumpets and crown vetch formed whole stretches of reds and pinks.

To Suzy's surprise, those separate patches continued moving among themselves, combining in places, creating various shades of color and a patchwork of designs, both regular and random, until she started detecting a recognizable pattern. That patchwork blended, each individual flower blurring into the next until the effect was a soft and realistic representation of a young woman around twenty years old.

Her features were somewhat plain, but they were pleasant and easy to look at. She had sparkling blue eyes and shining auburn hair.

"Who are you?" she asked frankly. Her friendly expression and pleasant voice softened the bluntness of her abrupt inquiry.

"I'm Suzy Quinn," Suzy replied, only slightly surprised by the occurrence, having witnessed similar scenes before. "And you?"

"Melody," the young woman said with a smile. "Melody Martin." Then, her smile faded and her eyebrows came together, and she looked confused. "How is it that you're not afraid of me?"

"Should I be afraid of you?" Suzy asked.

"It seems that not many people can see me," Melody replied, "but those who do are usually afraid."

"Well, I don't really see you," Suzy said, "I'm just dreaming." She knew she was nit-picking. For Suzy, first contact was usually made through a dream. "Besides, you just don't seem scary to me," Suzy said with a smile.

Melody smiled in return, an expression that seemed to come quite readily to her. It occurred to Suzy that Melody's vivacious way and easy smile made her appear prettier than she had originally thought.

"I'm so happy to meet someone who will actually talk to me, instead of avoiding me." Melody's bubbly personality was infectious, and Suzy found herself drawn to her.

"Do you live here?" Suzy asked, realizing the mistake in her phraseology when Melody's face darkened.

"I don't live anywhere," she said. "But I died here."

"I'm so sorry," Suzy replied.

"It's my own fault," Melody said, shaking her head as a more pleasant expression gradually returned to her face.

"You know," Suzy ventured carefully, "you don't have to stay here. You could move on, if you wanted to."

Melody shrugged her shoulders in an expression of youthful ambivalence.

"I like it here," she said, looking around. In that instant, Suzy realized that she wasn't outside anymore, but was in her room at the B&B. "I had some pleasant times here."

Melody's wistful expression stayed in Suzy's mind as she drifted deeper into sleep.

§

Her body still tuned to east coast time, Suzy woke early. She got quietly out of bed and found a spot on the floor where she had room to do some yoga poses. She stretched herself into a few positions, then settled in the lotus position, wishing she had a candle.

In the past year and a half, most of the times she had attempted contact, to view visions of the lives of ghosts, or what she called episodes, a flame had been the catalyst. The very first time it happened, before she realized she even had the ability, it had happened when she was staring into a candle flame, although she had used a gas fireplace on one occasion.

One time, it had happened without her even trying, while staring into the flame of a candle. That had been a little embarrassing, considering all the people around.

This morning, though, she realized that she had become quite adept at making contact, and it appeared that the candle wasn't necessary. It was still fairly dark in the room, but what details Suzy could see began to blend and blur, swirling into a different scene in a different setting.

4

Upon meeting Melody Martin for the first time, the average person might get an inkling of how her parents felt about music. If her sister, Harmony, was present as well, that inkling would likely deepen. The fact is that music was of utmost importance to their parents, and their children's names were just two of the results.

Jeremiah Martin had been a well-known and much sought-after violinist in New York City, playing in many venues in the Upper East Side, and in the burgeoning Upper West Side. Equally adept at fiery flamboyance and warm, heartfelt romanticism, he loved the classics.

It was in advance of one of his performances that he met his wife, Penelope. A sweet-voiced soprano, she had been engaged to sing selections from several Mozart operas while Jeremiah played violin and a mutual friend played piano.

Musically, Penelope was more serious than Jeremiah, and while she would sing secular music, her preference was for the Baroque sacred music of Praetorius and Gabrieli.

Their whirlwind romance became the talk of the town, and their wedding was attended by numerous well-known personages, including Mayor Hoffman.

Melody was born in May of 1866, followed by Harmony in August of 1867. Complications during Harmony's birth, though, meant that no further offspring would result from Jeremiah and Penelope's union. Still, the two girls, being so close in age, grew up inseparable, with the pride and devotion of their parents focused on them.

Due to Melody's bubbly personality and her apparent ability to make anyone smile with her mere presence, Jeremiah often called her Sunshine. Harmony, though of a more sober demeanor than her sister, excelled in whatever she put her mind to, and gained the nickname Little Star. Together, they were the light of their parents' lives.

Naturally, the girls were raised with a deep appreciation of music. Melody took up the piano, while Harmony, being more like her mother, followed in her mother's musical footsteps as a singer. At their parents' insistence, they performed together at numerous functions at their home.

For the girls, though, music was simply a pastime. Harmony was quiet and shy, and more serious, while Melody was vivacious and lighthearted, and had a bit of a wild streak. To the dismay of their parents, they didn't pursue music with the seriousness and dedication that was required to succeed as professional musicians in the city.

The happy family was torn asunder in 1886, just after Melody turned nineteen years old. Jeremiah got sick during a cholera outbreak in their neighborhood, followed quickly by Penelope. They died a few hours apart.

Though the bulk of the estate went to Jeremiah's brother, James, Melody and Harmony each inherited some cash. During and after their grieving period, they repeatedly refused the offers of several relatives to take them in. They decided, instead, to go west, ignoring all the shocked and horrified expressions.

They both recognized that they had neither the talent nor the inclination to pursue music in New York, but Melody thought that the great western frontier sounded exciting. She had heard all her life about people heading west to strike it rich, or to start a new life.

Harmony required a little more convincing, but in the end, a new life sounded good to both of them. So, they impulsively threw in their lot with a large group traveling to Colorado.

§

"How precious did that grace appear," Harmony sang as she tended breakfast beside their little wagon, "the hour I first believed."

Melody plopped herself down on the ground, having returned from an early morning walk along the South Platte River, which their wagon train had been following. She was humming There is a Tavern in the Town, *but she stopped when Harmony scowled at her. Normally, Harmony's scowl might have been enough to get Melody to engage her in an argument, but this morning, she didn't feel like it.*

They had crossed the northeastern border of Colorado the day before. It really didn't look any different than the plains of Nebraska that they had been traversing the last several days. But the stories that Melody had heard about the wild land of Colorado were striking a romantic chord in her heart, and she didn't want to spoil it.

Harmony didn't seem to be feeling the romance that Melody felt. She seemed irritable most of the time, except when she was singing, so Melody let her sing whenever she felt like it, without interruption.

It had been a long and arduous journey, admittedly one that could have been less long and arduous. The Transcontinental Railroad had been completed about eighteen years before, and other railroads were now crisscrossing the country. But that didn't appeal to Melody's romantic sense of adventure like crossing America with their possessions stowed in a wagon. Admittedly, their little wagon had nowhere near the grandeur of the mighty Conestogas that crossed the plains in decades past.

But their journey was also not as fraught with danger, since the Indians had been run out. Wars with Indians were still being fought in the southwest, but in this part of the country, they had ended nearly twenty years before.

Still, it was a hard journey. Mr. Morgan, the wagon master, said that they had travelled about 1,600 miles. For Melody and Harmony, it had been almost entirely on foot, since they had a small wagon and only one horse to pull it. Some of the bigger outfits were pulled by teams of draft horses or oxen, but Melody decided that wouldn't be necessary for the few possessions they were taking with them.

Walking miles every day, cooking over a campfire, sleeping on the ground. It had grown old for Harmony very quickly. The trip was harder when they were both plagued by memories of their parents. For Harmony, singing helped her feel closer to her mother.

Her singing seemed to attract the attention of others in their group, as well.

"Miss, that's just about the prettiest sound I've ever heard," said the young man who had nervously approached them. His

clothes were overworn and dusty, like everyone else's in their wagon train, but he spoke with a polite and gentlemanly manner.

"Thank you," Harmony said shyly, blushing at the compliment. She looked down toward the skillet, apparently feeling self-conscious.

"My name's Taylor Tuttle," he said, holding his hat in his hand and pushing his dark hair back out of his face. Melody watched, amused, as Harmony stood up and managed a timid curtsy.

"Pleased to meet you, Mr. Tuttle," she said. "I'm Harmony Martin."

Melody pushed herself up off the ground and put her hand out.

"And I'm her sister, Melody."

Taylor Tuttle politely shook her hand, but his attention immediately went back to Harmony.

"Where are you ladies heading?" he asked. Harmony looked at her sister.

"Melody says she'll know it when she sees it."

Melody smiled blithely as Taylor Tuttle looked at her, a little befuddled.

"What about you, Mr. Tuttle?" Melody asked. "Where are you going?"

"Oh, me and my friend are going to Georgetown. We're going to try our hand at mining."

Suddenly alerted by the burning smell of the potatoes she was frying, Harmony quickly knelt back down to move the skillet.

"Well, good luck to you, Mr. Tuttle," Melody said. "It was very nice meeting you."

Taylor Tuttle nodded at Melody, and turning back toward Harmony, he nodded again, but deeper, almost a bow.

Melody noticed that Harmony, from her position down by the fire, looked after Taylor Tuttle for several seconds as he walked away.

§

"I still don't understand why you were so anxious to come out here," Harmony groused several days later as she and Melody walked alongside their little wagon. "Every place we've come to, they've said that the gold is all played out."

"Land sakes, Harmony," Melody exclaimed, kicking a rock ahead of her.

"Mama said you shouldn't use slang," Harmony replied. It was an old admonition.

"I didn't know the gold was all played out until we got here," Melody said, ignoring her scolding. "But there's plenty of silver now." Then, she shook her head in exasperation. "Besides, we didn't come out here to find our fortune. We could have had that back home. I wanted to find adventure, romance."

"I think my feet have had all the adventure they can stand," Harmony pouted. In the last couple of months since they left New York, the blisters had subsided and toughened, but her feet and legs were constantly sore. "And you had romance back at home. We both did. Billy Bradford asked me to marry him, and half of the Upper East Side wanted to marry you.

Melody cast a disparaging sidelong glance at her sister, her lip curled in disdain.

"There was no adventure in that life. And little romance. You know we weren't cut out for life in the upper crust. Even with Mama and Papa, you remember how we often felt out of place. We were always being scrutinized and judged."

"I know," Harmony said reluctantly.

"And expected to perform."

Harmony pushed her blonde hair out of her face, tucking it back under her bonnet. She sighed, chagrined at how scraggly it looked.

"Still, I don't know why we couldn't have stayed back there in Georgetown. It seemed like a nice place."

"It was *nice," Melody agreed. She looked at her sister and nodded. "And we can always go back there if we decide we want to. It's only a couple of hours away. But I just want to see what Silver Plume is like."*

As they made their journey, their group had gradually changed, growing and shrinking as families and individuals joined them or broke away to settle in places along the way. Taylor Tuttle and his friend had stayed in Georgetown, as he had said, and though Harmony never said anything, she had been in a funk ever since then.

Melody had been tempted to break off and stay in a couple of places herself. Like Denver City. That was certainly a bustling place! But in the end, it seemed to her like just an adolescent version of New York, and she decided it wasn't for her.

Georgetown, too, had its appeal. But overall, it just didn't answer her need for adventure and romance. She wasn't sure what it would take to answer that need. She hoped she would recognize it when she saw it.

§

Leaving their wagon under the supervision of the wagon master, Mr. Morgan, Melody and Harmony wandered off from their group to explore Silver Plume. As they walked along the wooden sidewalk, which proved to be of a sporadic nature, the doors to the Grizzly Bar saloon suddenly swung open, hitting Melody in the face.

"Land sakes!" she cried as she slapped her hands up against her nose. The door would have struck her harder if it had not been stopped abruptly by the hand of a man approaching it from her left, directly in front of the door. A moment after the door swung open, another man staggered out of the saloon, apparently oblivious to what had just happened.

The man who caught the door, though, was very attentive. He let the door swing shut again, and he lifted his bowler hat from his head.

"Oh, my goodness, miss," he exclaimed with a vaguely English accent, "I'm so sorry this happened. Please, come inside and allow me to attend to your nose."

Melody felt a little unsteady, more from the shock and surprise than from pain, though she noticed that her nose was bleeding. Harmony had her by the arm, helping to steady her, and the man took her other arm.

"I hate to suggest it," he said, "but please come inside and we'll get that taken care of."

He pushed the door open, helping her into the saloon. It was early in the afternoon. Aside from a man at the bar and two at a table, the saloon was empty. The man and Harmony guided her into a chair at one of the empty tables, and the man went to the bar.

He returned quickly, followed by a saloon girl carrying a bowl of water.

"This is Husky Hannah," he said. "She said she'll be happy to take care of you."

"Thank you, sir," Harmony said. The man nodded and went back to the bar.

As 'Husky Hannah' dabbed at Melody's nose with a wet cloth, Melody, embarrassed by the debacle, tried to hear the conversation at the bar.

"Good afternoon, Mr. Griffin," the large and formidable man behind the bar said. "What'll you have?"

"I've not come for a drink, Griz," the Englishman said. "As you know, tomorrow is the fourth of July. I've come to pay my men's bar tabs."

"Ah, Mr. Griffin, you're a good man."

"Oh, I don't know about that. I just want to do what I can for my people."

Griz, pulled a worn ledger up from behind the bar, and they started going through it together.

Melody had her head back, and Husky Hannah got the blood cleaned from her face as the bleeding gradually stopped. Melody had been a little shocked and scandalized the first time she had contact with a saloon girl, somewhere in Ohio. Now, though, she saw Husky Hannah as just another woman, and a kind and helpful one at that.

"Thank you, Hannah," she said, sitting up. She didn't feel right calling attention to the woman's weight or physical appearance.

"You're welcome, miss." Husky Hannah smiled at her, wearing a bit of a surprised expression at Melody's civil treatment of her. Having finished his business with Griz, the Englishman now approached Melody and Harmony.

"Well," he said, "you look as good as new. I hope you're not in too much pain."

"No, sir," Melody replied, "it's not too bad. Thank you so much for your help."

"My pleasure. Clifford Griffin at your service, miss."

"I'm pleased to meet you, Mr. Griffin. I'm Melody Martin, and this is my sister, Harmony."

"What lovely, euphonious names," Griffin replied, smiling behind his dark mustache.

"Thank you," Melody said, smiling back at him, feeling a little sore as she did. She might have to try not smiling as much for a day or two.

"Might the two of you be as musical as your names would imply?"

"Jeremiah and Penelope Martin were our parents," she said. She didn't know if anybody would have heard of them out here, but Griffin's eyes lit up.

"Why, I heard them play at Gilmore's Garden!" he exclaimed enthusiastically. "Although as I understand it they're calling it Madison Square Garden now. But your parents were splendid! Your father was a great inspiration for me! And the two of you are their progeny?"

"I play piano," Melody said, hoping to avoid talking about her parents. "Harmony sings." Harmony curtsied.

"Ah," Griffin said, raising his dark eyebrows. "Are you, by any chance, seeking employment?" Melody and Harmony glanced at each other, then looked back at Griffin, unsure whether they should be suspicious or not. "I'm asking because Griz over there, the owner of the Grizzly Bar, lost his piano player, Charlie, a few days ago."

"I'm so sorry," Harmony said sympathetically.

"Oh, please don't worry yourself, Miss Harmony," Griffin said, smiling at her. "Charlie didn't die, he just left. Mining towns are strange things. People can be transient around here. They come and go."

Melody and Harmony looked at each other again, a questioning look in their eyes. They hadn't used up all the money they had inherited, by any means. They still had a sizable portion of it. But they had heard the story of how their father had scraped and saved before he got his first break. From this, they had learned the importance of frugality and saving. And they knew that their inheritance wouldn't last forever.

"Are we staying here?" Harmony asked.

Melody glanced at Griffin and felt a strange feeling in her stomach. While performing in New York hadn't appealed to her, the thought of playing in a mining town in the Colorado Rocky Mountains held a strange appeal. She looked back at Harmony and nodded.

"Yes, Mr. Griffin, I think we might be in need of both a job and a place to live."

"I may be able to help you on both counts," he replied. He turned to the bartender. "Griz," he called, "I believe I may have found your new entertainment."

§

Melody gazed down at the keyboard in front of her. She had never played an upright piano before but, despite the higher profile of the body of the instrument, she decided that the keyboard looked the same, though this one was decidedly more worn than any she had played. She looked up at Harmony, who had been doing some vocal exercises to warm up. Raising their eyebrows nervously at each other, they each nodded, and Melody began playing a simple tune.

Longing for Spring, an English translation of a beginner's song by Mozart, seemed a good start at the time. The piano part and the vocals were forgiving, assuming the performers had some talent, which Melody and Harmony did, especially considering how long it had been.

But Griz cast a doubtful look at Griffin. Melody saw that look and abruptly stopped playing. With Harmony's vocals interrupted, she looked at Melody inquiringly.

"I'm sorry, ladies," Griz said. "This ain't a New York concert hall. I gotta admit, you definitely got talent, but I'm afraid this ain't what I'm looking for. Can you play anything a little more lively?"

Melody and Harmony consulted briefly, then began performing Habanera *from* Carmen. *Once again, Griz shot that look at Griffin. Melody and Harmony stopped performing again, and Griffin stepped in.*

"Bizet is wonderful," he quickly interjected. "I love his music, myself. And who doesn't like Mozart? But I'm afraid Griz is right. I'm afraid the Grizzly Bar is a far cry from Madison Square Garden, and his clientele is not quite the right audience for classical music." He put on a hopeful expression. "Can you play anything a little more popular?"

Melody looked up at Harmony with a mischievous smile on her face. Growing up, she had been scolded numerous times for playing some of the music that had gained popularity among the masses. She loved playing it, but her mother said it was vulgar.

She started playing a bouncy rendition of Camptown Races. *Harmony, having less of the wild streak that her mother had scolded Melody about, was not as familiar with this music, though she and Melody had dabbled a bit. They followed that with* I'll Take You Home Again, Kathleen, *and finished with* Funiculì, Funiculà.

By the time they finished, Griz was smiling.

"When can you start?"

The girls stammered a bit until Griffin came to their rescue again.

"I'll get them set up with a place to live so they can get settled." He turned to the sisters. "Can you start tomorrow night? It's the fourth of July," he added with a cautious tone. "It will be rowdy."

"Land sakes!" Melody replied, her eyes shining. "It sounds wonderful!"

After they worked out the details regarding pay and what time to be there, they said goodbye to Griz. From there, Griffin led them down the street to a large and attractive new house festooned with gingerbread trim a couple of blocks away. Stepping up on the porch, he knocked on the door. A few seconds later, the door swung open.

Cordelia Watkins was once an attractive woman. It's not that the bloom of youth had passed and left her in its wake. She was only a few years older than Melody. But the savage scar that slashed down the right side of her face, along with the cane she leaned on, gave her an older, hardened look. Part of that look could be attributed to the fact that the scarred side of her face was not as expressive as the left side.

Her expression softened, though, when she saw Griffin.

"Hello, Clifford," she smiled.

"Good afternoon, Cordelia," Griffin smiled. "We were wondering if you might have a vacancy."

"I have a couple of them," she replied. "But I'm afraid I don't have one that would comfortably accommodate three. Who're your friends?"

"Oh, no," Griffin sputtered, putting his hands up in front of him. There was something akin to terror showing in his eyes. "You misunderstand. The room will be for these two young ladies, not for myself." Cordelia's subtle smile and nod indicated that she hadn't misunderstood. Griffin seemed to realize at that point that he had fallen for her joke. His sigh implied that it wasn't the first time.

"This is Melody and Harmony Martin," he introduced, his face red, and the girls smiled their greetings. "They've just arrived in town from New York. They're the new musicians down at the Grizzly Bar."

"Oh, so Griz finally replaced Charlie? Good for him. Come on in." She held the door open.

"I'm afraid I can't stay. I still have a few more saloons to visit," Griffin replied.

"Of course you do," Cordelia said with a warm smile. "It's July 3rd."

"Yes," he said, and he turned toward Melody and Harmony, "so I'll leave you ladies in Cordelia's capable hands."

"Thank you so much, Mr. Griffin," Melody said. Harmony offered her thanks as well, and Griffin smiled.

"It's been my pleasure. Good day." He tipped his bowler hat at the three of them and turned away.

"Well, come in, ladies. Let's get you settled." She stumped down a short, dark hallway, with Melody and Harmony following close behind. "I hope you'll forgive my saying so, but you both seem rather unseasoned to be out here in the mountains all by yourselves. This can be a rough and difficult place. Are your parents here with you?"

"No," Melody replied, "they've passed on."

"Oh, I'm so sorry," Cordelia said as she stopped and turned, looking at them for a moment, her strawberry blonde hair draped over one shoulder. Then, she turned and continued on her way. "Do you each want a room of your own, or do you both want to stay in the same room?"

Melody looked over her shoulder at Harmony, raising her eyebrows in a question.

"Same," Harmony said quietly.

As Cordelia turned, they each lifted their skirts a bit to negotiate the steep, dark staircase near the back of the house.

"So, you're both musicians?" Cordelia asked.

"Yes, I play piano," Melody said, "and Harmony sings."

"Judging by your names," Cordelia replied as she opened a door at the top of the stairs, "your parents must have had a high regard for music as well."

"Yes," Harmony replied quietly. The loss of their parents was still a difficult subject.

"Well, this is the more spacious of the two rooms I have available." They went into the room and looked around.

It was a simple room, with a pine bed, a pine wash stand and a pine wardrobe. Beside the window, two chairs stood at an angle from each other, with a small pine table between them.

"For the two of you, room and board is a dollar and a quarter a week, paid in advance," Cordelia said. "The rate for the other room is a little less, but it's also a little smaller, and not furnished quite as nicely."

Melody glanced at Harmony and, as they often did, they seemed to reach an unspoken agreement.

"I think this will be fine," Melody nodded. She opened her small beaded handbag and counted out the coins into Cordelia's

hand. Cordelia smiled and dropped the coins into a pocket in her apron.

"You have a very nice house," Harmony said. "What does your husband do?"

"Not much," Cordelia replied, leaning on her cane. "He's been gone for about three years."

"I'm so sorry," both girls said.

"I had just put some tea on before you showed up," Cordelia said cheerfully, abruptly. She seemed a little anxious to change the subject. "Would you ladies like a cup?" Both girls' faces brightened at the offer.

Back downstairs, Melody and Harmony shared a settee. The parlor was on the east side of the house and, in the afternoon, was a little cooler. Cordelia poured the tea and sat in a chair opposite them.

"Were the two of you friends of Clifford's in New York?" she asked.

"No," Melody replied, "we only met him about an hour ago. Is he from New York?"

"Well, he came out here from New York. His father is English, but Clifford may have been born and raised in New York or England. I'm not really certain of his place of origin. At any rate, he and his brother, Heneage, moved out here a few years ago, from New York City. Clifford is the manager of the 7:30 mine."

"The 7:30 mine?" Harmony echoed.

"A silver mine up the mountain," Cordelia replied, hooking a thumb over her shoulder. "It's called that because they start the shift at 7:30 in the morning, about an hour later than other mines in the area. It's not easy to get to. It's a rugged hike up a long path up the mountain, and Clifford is known around these parts as a very considerate man. He always takes good care of his people."

"You're the second one I've heard today who mentioned something about it being July 3, in relation to Mr. Griffin," Melody said.

"Yes, every year, before Independence Day, he settles up the bar tabs of the men who work for him. He wants them to be able to celebrate without using up their families' means. And every

Christmas, he purchases a goose for each of his employees for their Christmas dinners."

"How generous!" Harmony said.

"Yes," Cordelia agreed, "Clifford is an extremely charitable and benevolent man."

From the look on Cordelia's face and the softened tone of her voice, Melody wondered if her feelings for Griffin went deeper than simply admiration of his generosity. And as she listened to Cordelia's praises of him, she felt an odd, nervous feeling in her stomach.

5

"There you are," Fin said as his face came into focus. It was light in the room now, and she could see that he had a somewhat relieved smile on his face. He was sitting cross-legged on the floor in front of her. "Were you seeing an episode?"

Suzy nodded, taking a deep breath. It had been a while since she had done this, and it took a few moments for her to get past the fatigue and disorientation. She looked at Fin through narrowed eyelids.

"Did you know there was a ghost here when you booked the reservation?" she asked suspiciously.

"No, I didn't," Fin replied quickly. He sat up straight and put his right hand up as if he were being sworn in at court. "Honest."

Suzy looked at him skeptically. The right side of his mouth went up in a sort of half smile.

"Honey, considering that, when you're seeing your episodes, I'm basically alone, why would I do that, especially when you've already said you don't want to spend your time sending ghosts into the great beyond?"

"Well, to be fair, I said that after I got here. So you have an out this time."

"Still, I had no idea," Fin insisted.

Looking at the clock on the bedside table, Suzy saw that this episode had lasted nearly forty-five minutes. She struggled to push herself up, and Fin quickly stood. He took her hand and helped her to her feet.

"So, who is this ghost?" Fin asked.

"She's this very sweet girl named Melody Martin," Suzy replied.

"A sweet girl," Fin echoed. "Good. I'm hoping that I can be a little less wimpy about your ghosts this time. I think it might be easier to manage that with a sweet girl than with a bunch of crazed killers." Fin had been pretty frightened in the Edinburgh vaults when confronted by the ghosts of numerous people who had been killed there, and especially when he was completely engulfed by the ghost of one of their killers.

"I've also met – or rather Melody met Cordelia Watkins, the owner of the boarding house back then," Suzy continued. "I assume that's Dolores' great-grandmother." She looked at Fin. "This place is called Mountain Melody, right?"

"Yeah, that's right."

"I wonder why it was named after Melody instead of Cordelia."

"Maybe it was just an amazing coincidence. Like me booking a room in a B&B that has a ghost." He put his hand up again, to reinforce his claim.

"Did you have anything planned for today?"

"Nothing specific. Just sightseeing. Not that there's much to see in Silver Plume, but a drive through the mountains is always nice."

Suzy looked at him a little sheepishly.

"Do you mind if we spend the day in the room? I'm curious about this girl."

"That's fine," Fin replied, not quite convincingly considering the sigh that came out with the words. "I brought my computer with me. I can write while you're doing that. Assuming I can think of something to write."

"Thank you," Suzy said with a kiss on his cheek as a consolation prize. "And let's not say anything about Melody at breakfast. Let's just see if Dolores says anything about her."

The B&B was full and Dolores was kept busy at breakfast. She didn't have time for visiting much.

6

Take –" Melody watched Harmony as she held the E flat, repeating the arpeggio of the chord on the piano, until Harmony did a glissando from 'take' up to 'heart' in A flat. At that point, Melody concluded Poor Wandering One *with a flourish. They had quickly found that, if the tune was happy or playful, and especially if it was in English, the often rowdy patrons, consisting primarily of Colorado miners, didn't seem to mind if it was from a Gilbert and Sullivan opera.*

Melody had been a little surprised, though. She expected to be providing background music for the noisy saloon. But after only one or two songs, it seemed as if the majority of the patrons had turned to watch and listen, as if Melody and Harmony were the reason they were there.

Melody found that she enjoyed playing at the Grizzly Bar more than any of the performances that she had been compelled by her parents to do. Getting paid for it may have played a part in that, but the performance itself was more pleasant here, as well. Playing for the pompous folks that her parents often fraternized with always left her feeling studied and evaluated. Here, nobody was judging them. Nobody criticized their performance. They just enjoyed it.

Harmony seemed to enjoy it, as well. Though she was shy, she had always been able to throw herself into her performance. Singing brought her out of her shell. Still, she tended to keep her eyes closed much of the time, something their mother had counseled her on frequently.

Here, though, with the more casual atmosphere and audience, Melody noticed that Harmony was looking around as she sang, smiling, and apparently making eye contact.

After they finished Poor Wandering One, *an overenthusiastic patron with a few drinks under his belt rushed forward, attempting to get to the sisters. Harmony cowered against the piano, but her eager fan was prevented from making contact by Griz who had stationed himself nearby. Griz pushed the man back and stood between him and the sisters with his ponderous arms crossed.*

The miners and others who frequented the establishment were not accustomed to seeing two pretty young ladies in the rough saloon, and Griz found that the behavior of the general clientele seemed to improve a bit. Of course, there were some, like this man who had overindulged, whose conduct sometimes required adjustment, but for the most part, the girls were treated with respect.

Melody took it in stride, and was more amused than frightened when someone did or said something crude. Her mother, of course, would have been outraged and horrified at the crude behavior of these people. Harmony was too, occasionally, but Melody loved their new-found popularity.

After they finished the next song, the saloon again erupted in applause. As happy customers ordered more drinks from the bar, keeping Nick, the bartender busy, the noise in the saloon once again raised to a more cacophonous level. But Melody knew that the noise would die down at least a little with the opening notes of the next song. As she looked around, she saw Griz pushing through the crowd from the bar, carrying two glasses of sarsaparilla for them.

"Mr. Griffin," he said with surprise, as he encountered Griffin approaching the sisters, applauding enthusiastically, "I ain't known you to be down here in town on an evening in quite some time."

"Right you are, Griz," Griffin replied, smiling behind his mustache. "But I had to be here to witness Miss Melody and Miss Harmony's debut. And I must say it's been a pleasure. You young ladies played marvelously!"

"Thank you, Mr. Griffin," Melody said with a glowing smile. Harmony echoed her thanks.

"Griz," Griffin said, looking at the crowd in the little saloon, "you may have to add more seating and turn this into a concert hall."

"I'm just a drink slinger," Griz said with a shake of his head and a roll of his eyes. "I don't know nothin' about runnin' a concert hall."

"Well, from the look of the crowd at the bar, I'd say they're at least attracting more customers for you."

"They sure are. Speakin' o' which, Nick's lookin' a little beset. I better get back there and give 'im a hand." He turned toward the sisters. "You ladies really are doin' a fine job."

"Thank you, sir," they both replied as he hurried back to the bar.

"I must be on my way, as well," Griffin said. "It will be dark soon, and I have a trek to get to my home."

"We really do appreciate you helping us get this job," Melody said.

"You're more than welcome, I assure you. Your musicality is certainly doing your parents proud."

Harmony caught her breath at the mention of their parents. She looked down and dabbed away a sudden tear as Melody beamed at the remark.

"Goodnight, ladies," Griffin said, tapping his bowler hat on his head. Then, as if having an epiphany, he added, "Perhaps your next tune."

He smiled and waved, his gaze lingering for a few moments on Harmony, as he turned and pushed his way through the crowd.

"I think Goodnight Ladies should be our last song, don't you?" Melody asked. Harmony smiled and nodded, as they began the opening notes to Polly Wolly Doodle.

§

As Griz escorted Melody and Harmony down the dark street to Cordelia's boarding house, they heard a haunting melody wafting down from the mountain.

"Is that a violin?" Melody asked.

"Yeah," Griz replied softly, a little uncomfortably. He glanced up the black hulk of the mountain where the sounds were originating. But they were already at Cordelia's house, and Griz directed his attention to opening the front door for his two young charges.

"I'll see you girls tomorrow," he said.

"Good night, Griz," Harmony said, her eyes drooping. They closed the door behind them and went quietly down the dark hallway.

"So?" Startled, Melody turned and saw Cordelia, backlit by a light coming through the door to the kitchen. "How was your *opening night?" Harmony, coming down from her performance, seemed too exhausted to visit. She mumbled a goodnight and continued upstairs.*

"Land sakes, Cordelia, it was magnificent," Melody effused.

"Magnificent?" Cordelia echoed, disbelief blanketing her face. "I don't believe I've ever heard the Grizzly Bar described in such rhapsodic terms."

"I've never known such excitement, such praise."

"Do you want to talk about it?" Cordelia asked, motioning to the table and chairs in the dining room.

"I don't feel like I can sleep yet," Melody replied as she sat down in one of the chairs. She spent a couple of minutes describing the atmosphere in the saloon, the crowd, and how Griz had said he hadn't had as much business in the last week as he had in the last hour.

Cordelia smiled at Melody's excitement, but then Melody stopped. She looked at Cordelia, puzzled, as another thought came to mind.

"As we were walking home tonight, we heard violin music coming down from the mountain. Griz didn't seem to want to talk about it."

"Hmm," Cordelia said with a knowing nod, tracing the wood grain in the table top with her finger. "Men seem to have a hard time with anything that smacks of emotions." She looked up at Melody. "That was Clifford."

"Mr. Griffin? He plays the violin?"

"He does. He plays it every night." Leaving her cane hooked on the edge of the table, she pushed herself up and limped to the sideboard. She held up a bottle and raised her eyebrows in an unspoken question to Melody. Melody had never had spirits before, and she responded with a combination of a nod and a shrug. Cordelia poured two glasses and limped back, easing herself back down into her chair.

"Clifford was engaged to be married in New York," she continued, as Melody took a sip. The whiskey burned her mouth and her throat, but once it got past there, she realized that the effect was not entirely unpleasant. "His whole world revolved around

Olivia, and vice versa. Their union was not to be a matter of convenience, nor a business interest, nor about the merging of family fortunes. It was entirely about mutual love.

"Among the interests they shared, they both loved music. Clifford took her to concerts, and they even played together. He played his violin while she accompanied him on the piano. Not professionally, you understand, but just for their own personal enjoyment.

"But she became sick and died unexpectedly the day before they were to be married. Clifford was heartbroken. He was despondent for days. It was only when his brother, Heneage, insisted that they come out west to make a new start that he seemed to come out of it a bit. And it came to pass that it was a good start for both of them. Heneage saw opportunity out here, and they've been running the 7:30 mine ever since."

"But the music?" Melody asked.

"Yes, Clifford's still haunted by the love of his dead fiancée, and he can hardly bear to spend evenings in town, among crowds of men and women, reminding him of what he lost. He lives in a modest home up on the mountain, not far from the entrance to the mine. And every evening, he perches himself on a cliff overlooking the town, and he plays tunes that, I assume, he and Olivia once played together."

"But wouldn't that also remind him of what he lost?" Melody asked. Cordelia smiled wistfully.

"Where matters of the heart are concerned, Melody, people seldom do what might be considered the logical thing." She sighed and finished the last of her whiskey. "The acoustics of the valley are such that the sound from the cliff carries down into town for any who care to listen."

"So, he had to get back up there so he could play," Melody mused.

"'Get back up there?'" Cordelia asked.

"Yes, when we took a short break, he was very complimentary, but said that he had to get home."

"You're telling me that Clifford was there at the Grizzly Bar tonight?" Cordelia inquired, surprised. Melody nodded. "My

goodness, Melody, you ladies must have made quite an impression on him!"

§

Melody's adaptation to life in Silver Plume, and to playing for the crowds at the Grizzly Bar, was remarkable. Within a few days, Griz seemed to feel comfortable not standing guard over the sisters as they played.

The turning point, Melody thought, seemed to be when a rather inebriated regular approached them, his arms outstretched as if to embrace Harmony while she was singing. Before Griz could get to him, Melody lifted her leg to the side, planting her foot on his hip, and pushed him away, into the arms of a few surprised but laughing audience members, and never missed a note of My Old Kentucky Home.

Harmony seemed shocked at Melody's unladylike action, but was grateful nonetheless. From that moment on, having proved her fearlessness, Melody noticed that Griz, while still keeping a wary eye on his patrons, spent more time at the bar, a fact that Nick, the bartender, seemed to appreciate.

She had seen Griffin a couple more times among the throngs of people, and he always smiled and doffed his hat when he saw her. But he never spent much time in their company and, as he had that first evening, he always left before dark.

Invariably, they heard Griffin's violin music wafting down from the cliff as they made their way home. Melody had related his story to Harmony after that first night, and it always caused a pang in their chests when they heard it. It also reminded them of their father, which made it even more poignant for them.

But it was the time she spent with Cordelia after they got back home that Melody always looked forward to. Evenings in the saloon always tired Harmony so that she went straight up to bed. Melody, though, was always far too excited, too energized, to be able to sleep. So she invariably joined Cordelia for a glass of whiskey or port, or a cup of tea. The second time, they moved to the parlor to take advantage of the more comfortable seating, and that's where their custom continued. It was always the perfect end to the evening, allowing Melody to relax enough to be able to sleep.

"Mr. Griffin was there again this evening," Melody said, sipping her sweet wine and settling back into the settee in a way that would have had her mother scolding her. Cordelia, though, struck a similar pose on the other end of the settee, with her bad leg stretched out on the floor in front of her.

She took a sip as well and raised her eyebrows.

"I think the man may be infatuated."

"What?" Melody asked, startled. "You think he's attracted to Harmony?"

"Well, it's possible," Cordelia replied, a slight smile playing about her lips. "But, having witnessed the way his eyes lingered on you when he first brought you here, Melody, I believe you *may be the more likely object of his admiration." Melody's face wore a pensive expression as Cordelia continued. "And unless I'm seriously mistaken, I think his feelings might not be entirely unreciprocated."*

Melody remembered all the young men back in New York who had vied for her affection. None of them had appealed to her, at least beyond friendship. When she thought about Griffin, his kindness, his generosity, his maturity, she felt a warm feeling in her heart. She knew she could do a lot worse. She looked at Cordelia who was smiling at her over her glass.

"Land sakes, Cordelia, how do you know this?" Melody asked in a whisper.

"I'm a very wise and observant woman."

7

It was nearly two weeks before Griffin's feelings became known to others besides Cordelia. He called at the boarding house on a Sunday afternoon.

Melody and Harmony, along with a couple of other tenants, were finishing their tea in the parlor with Cordelia when there was a knock at the door. Cordelia turned and, reaching for her cane, started to stand.

"Don't trouble yourself," Melody said, patting Cordelia's shoulder. "I'll get it."

Opening the door, she saw Griffin standing there, his bowler hat in his hands.

"Oh, good afternoon, Mr. Griffin," Melody smiled. Griffin fidgeted nervously, nodding his head in a sort of bow.

"Uh, yes, good afternoon, Miss Melody," he stammered nervously. "How do you do?"

"I do very well, thank you. And you?"

"I – well, fine. Fine."

"Would you like for me to get Cordelia for you?" Melody asked.

"No. Actually, I've come to see you, Miss Melody." He took a moment and a breath, then looked squarely at her. "Miss Melody, I wonder if you might be interested in going for a walk."

Melody glanced over at Cordelia in the parlor. As she did, she felt an unsteady flutter in her stomach, and she took a breath of her own.

"A walk? Why yes, Mr. Griffin, that would be very nice." She turned toward Cordelia who was still sitting in the parlor and had overheard their exchange. She was smiling, the left side more than the right. She nodded her head and made a shooing motion with her hand.

Melody turned back toward Griffin, who patted his hat onto his head and stuck his elbow out. Melody pulled the door closed and put her hand through his arm, and they stepped off the porch onto the hot, dusty street.

They were both quiet for a while, speaking only to greet friends and acquaintances they passed. Melody noticed that some of the people they greeted looked curiously at them, some even displaying surprise or shock.

After a few moments, Griffin finally spoke.

"I'm sure you've likely noticed some of the looks we're receiving," he said. "I suppose I must explain."

Melody didn't know if she should let him know that Cordelia had already told her about his fiancée or not. She decided to keep quiet and listen to what he had to say.

"A few years ago, when I was a younger man, I was engaged to be married to a lovely girl in New York. Olivia was the light of my life, and I will happily admit that she seemed to adore me as well. But, sadly, the very day before our wedding, she died.

"The cause of death was ruled to be of natural causes, although for one so young and vibrant, there was nothing at all natural about it."

"Mr. Griffin," Melody said, wishing now that she had saved him the telling, "I'm so sorry."

"Thank you," he said with a glancing smile in her direction. "But ever since then, I've tended to keep to myself. I suppose you probably noticed Griz' reaction to seeing me in his saloon when you started playing there. Most evenings, I sit on a cliff near the entrance to my mine and play my violin. You may have heard it when you made your way home from the Grizzly Bar."

"I have," Melody replied. "It's lovely."

"Well, the point is that people around here are not accustomed to seeing me out and about, especially with a pretty young lady on my arm." Melody smiled and blushed. "So the fact that I've, well, taken an interest in you is something quite noteworthy."

"I understand, Mr. Griffin."

Griffin looked at Melody for a moment as they continued.

"Given our current situation of increasing intimacy, I hope that I might persuade you to call me Clifford. Although," he quickly added, "I do not mean to compel you toward a deeper intimacy if it is not something that you wish to pursue."

"I appreciate your concern, Clifford," Melody said, savoring the name, and unconsciously squeezing his arm a bit, "but I must confess that I have felt a certain affection toward you, as well."

Griffin smiled behind his mustache and, without thinking, he stood a bit taller.

After walking around a couple of blocks, they found themselves back in front of the boarding house. Melody thought that Griffin seemed a bit disappointed, but he smiled at her, a little more confidently now, and escorted her up onto the porch.

"Well, Miss – Melody," he said with a nervous smile, "uh, do you enjoy nature?"

"I admit I've not had much exposure to it, aside from passing through it on the way from New York. But the views around here are exceedingly fine."

"Perhaps another time I might show you around the forest," Griffin replied. "I am most fond of the natural wonders to be found in this area."

"That sounds very nice, Clifford."

"Until next time," Griffin said, and he took her hand and bent over, kissing it softly. Melody saw Cordelia peek out the window, and that unsteady feeling reappeared in her stomach, spreading upwards, resulting in a pink blush on her cheeks.

§

"Sarsaparilla's alright," Melody said, her voice soft and imploring, "but I'd rather have a glass of whiskey." Griz looked at her from under sternly-set eyebrows. Finally, he shook his head and poured a glass.

"Cordelia Watkins has been a bad influence on you," he said, and he placed the glass in front of her.

"Thank you, Griz," she beamed, taking the glass with her and heading back toward the piano. As she approached, she was surprised to see Harmony speaking with a young man. She wasn't nearly as outgoing as Melody, and it wasn't often that she engaged in conversation with someone, especially not as happily and pleasantly as she seemed to be doing so now.

As Melody came closer, she saw the man's face. It was the young man who had taken an interest in Harmony on the way west, but had stayed in Georgetown.

"Land sakes," she said as she came around to the stool in front of the piano, "Taylor Tuttle. Fancy meeting you here."

"Hello, Miss Melody," he said, smiling.

"He came specifically to see me," Harmony said, a little flustered.

"Is that so?" Melody took a sip of her whiskey. Tuttle looked at her a moment before responding. Melody couldn't tell if he disapproved of a woman drinking whiskey, but she didn't spend any time pondering it.

"Yes, miss," he said. "A buddy of mine spoke of a new singer at the Grizzly Bar, a pretty young blonde who sang like an angel, and I wondered if it might be Miss Harmony. I had to come and see for myself."

"How was it you came to think that it could be Harmony?" Melody asked.

"I just remembered hearing Miss Harmony singing while she was making your breakfast in the mornings on the way out here." He looked at Harmony with an adoring smile. "It really was the voice of an angel."

"Well, I'm sorry we're not going to be doing an angelic song next," Melody said.

"Whatever it is, it will sound angelic when Harmony sings it," Tuttle replied, completely undaunted.

"Yes, it will," Melody agreed with a smile toward her sister, taking another sip and sitting down on the stool. As Tuttle looked back at Harmony, he returned to his table as Melody began playing the first notes of My Grandfather's Clock.

§

"Where is your mine, Clifford?" Melody asked as she followed Griffin along a trail through the forest, not far from the edge of town. "I think I should like to see it."

"Oh, Melody, It's up the mountain, at the end of a steep trail nearly two miles long," Griffin replied with an admonishing tone. "I would not advise it. There's really nothing to see, anyway. It's just a hole in the mountain. Although the view from that vantage point is quite splendid."

"I love that you play your violin up there. You share your gift with everyone in the town."

"It's nothing," he replied humbly.

"No, don't say that. It's wonderful. My father was the same way. He loved to share his gift with others. Although he usually got paid for it."

"Obviously a smarter man than I am." Griffin smiled.

He suddenly stopped and pointed at two vivid hummingbirds hovering not far from them, feeding on the nectar from a clump of white flowers. The scattered dapples of sunlight through the foliage overhead would occasionally catch the brilliant green plumage and ignite it into a sparkling fire.

"Oh!" Melody exclaimed, clasping her hands together. "How lovely they are!"

"Some of the Indians who used to live in the area," Griffin said, now speaking barely above a whisper, "considered the hummingbird to be sacred. Some viewed them as healers, or as messengers or incarnations of the dead."

Melody felt a brief pang of longing at his remark as she watched the busy little birds, and she placed her hands over her heart at the thought.

"Do you think they might be my parents?" she asked softly.

"Uh, well," Griffin stammered, "I wasn't saying that's what they are, I was simply stating what a primitive people believed."

"I think it's a lovely belief."

"Besides, those are both males." He seemed to catch the disappointed look on Melody's face, and he quickly added, "Although messengers, or incarnations, I suppose, don't have to be the same gender as those who sent them."

Melody smiled at him, and looked back quickly as the birds flew away, their wings making a loud buzzing sound.

"Have you ever seen any?" Melody asked as she turned back to Griffin.

"Any what?"

"Any real Indians."

"Ah, yes, I have. There were still a few around here when I first arrived. They used to be a proud and mighty people, from what I hear. They may have had quaint beliefs, perhaps, from our civilized and enlightened standpoint. Like the hummingbirds, for example. But they held the earth in high regard. They lived amicably with

nature instead of conquering and taming it as we white people feel the need to attempt.

"Now," he looked thoughtfully into the distance, "they are, I think, a mere shadow of what they once were. Those who are left, we've pushed west and south of here. The land there is not as useful to us and we care less about it. So, in our benevolence, we've reserved it for them.

"The last ones I saw," he looked back at Melody, pondering, "well, they were real *Indians, but I don't know how authentic they were. They were traveling with Buffalo Bill's Wild West Show. He seemed to treat them with respect, but still it was after they had been beaten down by the white man. By this time, they seemed little more than a novelty to be displayed for our amusement."*

"You're such a caring man," Melody said tenderly.

"I do care about people," he replied, as if it was only natural. "I care about whether they have what they need, whether they're treated well, whether they're happy." He looked around as if regaining awareness of his surroundings. "And I care what people might say if I don't get you back soon."

"Oh, land sakes," Melody said with a wave of her hand, "people will say what they say."

"Be that as it may," he replied with a slightly reproving smile, "I do not wish to be the reason for any unsavory rumors which might begin circulating about you and your purity. We should get back."

8

When Suzy emerged from her trance, blinking her surroundings back into focus, she was alone in the room. The bathroom door was open, so she knew Fin wasn't in there. She was about to go looking for him when the door to the room opened.

"There you are," Suzy said as Fin walked in.

"Oh, you're back." He sat down on the edge of the bed, tenderly stroking her thigh. "I didn't know if my being on the phone would interfere with your episode."

"I had people talking to me and shaking me in a panic last year when I went into an episode in front of the Daughters of the American Revolution. Despite their panic, I didn't come out of it until I was ready. Or until Fiona was. What's up?"

"It was just my agent," Fin replied, shaking his head, as he slipped his phone back in the holster on his belt. "He was updating me on the progress of *A Place Made of Time.* They've completed the first draft of the screenplay."

"Congratulations," Suzy smiled.

"Thanks. But it's not news that I needed to be updated on. I think he's just hoping the news will spur me on to actually starting a follow up."

"Hmm. And still nothing on that front?"

"Well, actually, I've been toying with an idea, and I wanted to run it past you. A while back, it was suggested to me that I do a ghost story. What do you think about being my muse?

"Your muse?" Suzy replied, pondering, looking at Fin through narrowed eyelids. "Yeah, I can do that. I can kick your ass now and then."

"No, you don't understand," Fin said a little uneasily, "I need a muse, not a slave driver."

"You need motivation."

"I need inspiration."

"And a kick in the ass now and then."

"You know," Fin said, standing and walking around to his side of the bed, "on further contemplation," he sat down next to her against the headboard, "I think I'm going to change the job title. I don't need a muse. Or a literary tyrant. So what I'm thinking about is using you for my very own personal idea quarry."

"Idea quarry? Really? That sounds a lot less sexy than muse."

"Sorry, babe. Seriously, though, I have so much material available to me with the stories you've told me about your contact with various ghosts."

"So, what are you thinking about?"

"Well," he pondered, "there's plenty of romance and potential pathos with the story of, what was his name? Jimmy Campbell?"

"In the hotel in Edinburgh," Suzy replied. "Right."

"Right, dying in the hotel room with his new bride, just before he was to be shipped out to fight in World War I. Quite a story. But all we know is what he told you in that brief contact you had with him. Not a lot of information to go on."

"True," Suzy nodded, as her face took on its signature smartass expression, "but any writer worth his salt might be able to construct his own story from those few details as prompts."

"I never claimed to be worth salt," Fin replied offhandedly. "Then there was Jill Bruch. I know there's a fair amount of information available on her, with your personal knowledge about the case, and with all the newspaper articles. But still, no offense to her, but as a story, it's just a simple thriller with a fairly obvious outcome."

"Okay," Suzy said, "so that leaves Fiona and Melody."

"Right. And my last novel was set in Edinburgh. Fiona's story really was fascinating, and I may come back to it someday. But for now, I think it would be really cool to write a story based in my own state. I mean Stephen King does it all the time."

"So, you're thinking about Melody's story?"

"Maybe. I mean, I'll have to see how it turns out. If it's as interesting as Fiona's story."

"Of course," Suzy said. "Well, let me catch you up."

9

Did you hear that new piece that Mr. Griffin played last night?" asked Charles Webb, one of the long-time tenants in the boarding house. He was speaking, as usual, to John Parker, another tenant. "The one directly following the Albinoni Adagio?" Both men were in their sixties, and they usually listened to Griffin's music through the open windows in their respective rooms, weather permitting. Sitting down to breakfast the next morning, the two men often discussed between themselves the previous evening's concert.

Melody had noticed that they seemed knowledgeable about music, and often used musical terminology in their discussions. She had never known them to play any instruments, but thought that they may have been musicians in their past. Being musicians themselves, Melody and Harmony often listened to their discussions, but on the occasions when they had asked questions about it, the men seemed a little flustered. Both men seemed very private, so the sisters generally left them to themselves.

"I did," Parker replied effusively. "It was such a lovely adagio, and played with such espressivo and grazioso!"

"What did he play?" Melody asked, too curious this time to let it go. On her way home from the Grizzly Bar, she had heard the end of a sonata by Corelli and a violin concerto by Bach wafting down from the cliff. But she hadn't heard anything new that sounded like what they were describing.

The men turned toward her, a little surprised to be asked.

"Uh, well," Webb stammered, "I honestly have no idea what it might be." He looked at Parker for confirmation. Parker shook his head.

"We've never heard it before," Parker said. "But it was such an exquisite melody."

"It was indeed," Webb added. "And the way it echoed off the walls of the valley, as they all do, of course, only added to the tonal quality of the piece."

Melody was surprised at their enthusiastic response, given how private they usually were.

"It's interesting," Parker said thoughtfully, "we've both observed in the past that Mr. Griffin usually plays melancholy music, in a minor key. Certainly understandable, given his story, which I'm sure you've probably heard." Melody nodded. "But this piece actually sounded happy."

"Yes," Webb replied, "it did. Happy and hopeful."

"You know," Parker concluded, "I think this new 'mountain melody' has become a favorite of mine."

"Oh, yes," Webb agreed, "mine as well."

"Hmm," Melody replied. As she looked away from the men, she glanced at Cordelia, sitting across the table from her. She was smiling.

§

"Some of the tenants were talking about a new 'mountain melody' that you played last night," Melody said. Griffin had made it a point to take a few minutes before she and Harmony began their engagement at the Grizzly Bar to call on her. They were sitting on the front porch of the boarding house.

"'Mountain Melody,'" he repeated, mulling over the phrase. "I like that. I think that is what I shall call it. I was thinking of you, after all, when I composed it." He smiled. "You must thank them for me."

"I shall," Melody agreed. "You were thinking of me?"

"I find myself thinking of you quite often," Griffin said, thoughtfully, looking off into the distance. Melody sighed, but she saw something around his eyes that she couldn't quite identify. Perhaps some sadness lingering just beneath the surface.

"What is it, Clifford?" she asked softly.

He looked at Melody as if he had just remembered that she was there. Then, he shook his head and smiled.

"Oh, it's nothing, my dear." He seemed a little relieved when Harmony opened the door and came out on the porch.

"We should go," she said. Griffin stood and offered his hand to Melody, helping her to her feet.

"I shall try to time my performance a little better tonight," he said, "so that you can hear your Mountain Melody as you walk home."

"Thank you, Clifford," Melody replied, noticing that he was still holding on to her hand. She looked down at their hands, and Griffin took the hint.

"Oh, so sorry," he said quickly, releasing her hand. "You must go and so must I. I have a long trail to climb to my cliff."

Melody smiled at him as she and Harmony walked away.

10

"Do you know anything about a trail to the 7:30 mine?" Suzy asked Dolores.

"Oh, sure," Dolores replied, her eyes magnified behind her thick glasses. Fin couldn't help thinking of Professor Sybill Trelawney from the *Harry Potter* movies. She was busy making a blackberry compote for the next day's breakfast, but was happy to talk to them while she worked. "People hike that all the time. If you go north on Silver Street, follow it up to the end, the trailhead starts there."

"Trailhead?" Fin asked. "It's actually still an existing trail?"

"It is. It's a pretty good hike, though. I mean, if you're not accustomed to hiking trails marked moderate or higher," Fin was sure he saw her enlarged eyes glance down over their physique, "you'll want to give yourself a few hours to do it."

"Maybe we can do it tomorrow morning," Fin said, looking at Suzy.

"Thank you very much," Suzy said. Dolores smiled and nodded.

Leaving Dolores to her chore, Fin led Suzy outside to his car. They had skipped lunch while Suzy was engaged in viewing Melody's episodes, and they were hungry for an early dinner, which required driving three miles back to Georgetown.

"Dolores didn't seem too optimistic about us," Suzy said as they pulled away.

"Oh, you noticed that too, did you?" Fin asked. "Well, I've done a fair amount of hiking out here. I *am* a little concerned about you, though. You're not accustomed to the altitude."

"Thank you, AltiDood," Suzy replied. "I'll take it slower if necessary."

"Good," Fin said with a smile.

"I'm still amazed at this 'Main Street,' Suzy said as they drove through the little town toward I-70. "Unpaved, and I can practically count on one hand the number of businesses on the street."

"Yeah, well Silver Plume is called a living ghost town. There are several nice, quaint little homes, but they're often right next to empty, decrepit buildings."

"Is that why you decided to bring your ghost whispering girlfriend here?" Suzy asked, suspicious once again, but her suspicion was softened with a smile.

"Honey, the term 'ghost town' doesn't necessarily mean 'ghosts.' I just thought Silver Plume would give you a sense of the mountains and the history of Colorado, without having to drive too far into the high country."

"It *is* nice," Suzy conceded, "even the empty, decrepit buildings."

Cooper's on the Creek caught their eye once they got into Georgetown. They enjoyed good food, and even live music by a local guitar duo, in the back room right on Clear Creek. Fin thought it was interesting that, despite how little actual contact they had had throughout the day, while Suzy was involved in the episodes, they were both content to relax quietly, enjoying their food and the music, with only a minimum of talking.

When the duo took a break, Fin and Suzy glanced at each other and decided that they were ready to go.

"This is an electric car, right?" Suzy asked as they pulled onto the highway back toward Silver Plume.

"That's right," Fin replied.

"Don't you need to plug it in?"

"You obviously haven't heard about the Tesla enthusiasts in Denver. A couple of guys tried to drive more than six hundred miles on a charge. This was on a looped track near Denver International Airport, and it was at slower speeds, but still, they made it to 606.2 miles on a single charge. We've barely driven 75 miles."

"Geeks are so weird," Suzy said. Fin glanced at her, and he saw that, despite her remark, she seemed impressed by the information, and he grinned.

When they got back to Mountain Melody, relaxed and comfortably filled, they made love, after which Fin got ready to sleep while Suzy entered one last episode for the day.

11

"I don't know what to do," Melody said. She and Cordelia were relaxing in the parlor in front of a warm fire. Outside, fat flakes of snow, briefly illuminated by the firelight through the window, tumbled down from the sky.

She and Harmony did not have to work tonight, so Melody decided to relax at home, while Taylor Tuttle took Harmony out for dinner.

"Did he say he doesn't want to see you anymore?" Cordelia asked.

"No, not in so many words."

"Well, what words did *he use?"*

Melody sat pondering for a moment, her eyebrows pulled together in thought.

"He said he needs to step back for a bit." She looked at Cordelia. "What does that even mean?" Cordelia smiled.

"That's male *for 'I'm afraid and I don't know what to do.'"*

"What do you mean? Why is he afraid? And if he is, why can't he just say it? Sometimes I'm *afraid and don't know what to do. Like right now!"*

"Yes, but you're a woman. You're expected to be helpless and afraid. Yet despite that, you weren't afraid to say it just now. Men can't seem to utter those words. They have to be strong and save us from terrors within and without." Cordelia looked thoughtful again. "Did he say anything else that might point to what he's afraid of?"

"He mentioned his dead fiancée, and that he feels guilty showing me attention." Melody paused as she looked down at her hands folded in her lap. "I don't understand, Cordelia, she's been dead for years."

Cordelia shifted on her end of the settee, stretching her bad leg out in front of her.

"Do you still miss your parents?" she asked.

"Of course!"

"That's what love does," Cordelia nodded. "Clifford loved Olivia. That didn't end just because she died." She reached out

and put her hand on Melody's. "And it doesn't mean that he feels any less regard for you. He will likely always love her. You'll just have to be content knowing that there was somebody before you who made his heart beat."

Melody closed her hand over Cordelia's. She felt that unsteady sensation again in her stomach. Just from talking about him! She sighed and looked up at Cordelia.

"If you don't mind my saying so," Cordelia said, "despite your perplexity, you don't seem as distressed about this turn of events as I would expect."

"I don't know," Melody said, "I am *distressed. I'm just confused." She sighed and shook her head, turning to shift position herself. She looked up at Cordelia. "Were you ever interested in Clifford?"*

"Me? No," Cordelia said definitively.

"Why not? You're a smart and beautiful woman, you're a few years older than me, so you're closer to his age." Cordelia tried to contain the chortle that burst from her mouth.

"I'll ignore that last part," she said. "But you think I'm a beautiful woman? I think you might need to have your eyes examined." To reinforce her point, she turned her face toward Melody to show the scar slashed across the right side. For further emphasis, she held up her cane and gave it nimble twirl through her fingers.

"Yes, I'm aware of the scar and the cane," Melody argued gently. "They don't change the facts."

Illuminated only by the dim firelight, Melody couldn't tell for certain, but she thought Cordelia might have blushed at the compliment.

"I'm curious," Cordelia said, peering at Melody, "in the months that we've known each other, you've never once asked how I ended up in this condition."

Melody stared at the fire for a few moments.

"When I was a little girl, backstage after a concert, a man was talking with my parents, telling them how much he enjoyed their music. The man had only one arm and, being a little girl, I asked him where his other arm was. He was gracious about it and said that it was shot off by a Confederate soldier.

"My mother, though, corrected me about it later. She explained that it's not polite to ask personal questions about someone's appearance. So, I don't."

"Hmm, I keep forgetting you're polite. There's not a lot of that in a mountain mining town." Cordelia stared at the fire herself, as if steeling herself for her explanation. "My husband, Lee, was not *a polite man, nor was he kind. He used to hit me regularly, when he wasn't at one of the saloons drinking and gambling.*

"He had made a fortune on his mining claim. That's how he could build this big, fine house in town. After he acquired the house, and a wife to take care of it, his claim seemed to play itself out. He'd find occasional chips or nuggets of silver, but it appeared that his fortune had primarily come from a small, isolated vein.

"When the money wasn't coming in as regularly, I suggested the possibility of selling the house and getting a smaller one. We didn't need so much room for just the two of us. His response was to hit me, then drag me upstairs to our bedroom where he – well, he raped me."

Melody looked at Cordelia, horrified, feeling a lump in her heart for her friend.

"That was the beginning of his new agenda, to be enacted every week or two. In between those episodes, he would go to the saloons to gamble what money he did have, in hopes of making back his fortune. His plans rarely paid off, though, as he was not a very good gambler." A few quiet seconds passed.

"Meanwhile, I had found another . . ." Cordelia paused, her eyes filling up, as she tried to decide on the right word, "another person to give my affection to." She glanced at Melody, hesitant to continue. She took a deep breath and held it for a moment before blowing it out in a quick sigh. Before she started speaking, she looked away again, wiping her eyes. "The people who used to live next door, a gruff family, had a widowed daughter who visited me often. Jessie knew that Lee was not good to me, and she sympathized. She spent time here with me when he was not home.

"In time, we discovered that – well, that we could provide for each other the tenderness that we were both missing in our homes." As her meaning sunk in, Melody felt shocked, but she

tried to temper her expression when Cordelia ventured a glance at her. She didn't know if she succeeded. "We both knew it was wrong, but there was such a hole in both of our hearts that we each gladly gave what we could to each other, and we felt those voids filling up.

"Before we realized it, we had fallen in love. Jessie was everything I wanted but never knew. She was with me every day. Sometimes, we would go for a walk into the forest, to a private place, and we would make love. Other times, we would stay here, if I knew that Lee would be gone for a while.

"One day, though, I misjudged. Lee had, apparently, gotten tired of spending so much time working on a claim that was no longer yielding any silver, and he came back home early in the day. He found Jessie and me . . . in bed together.

"He pulled Jessie out of bed and hit her. He scooped up her clothes and dragged her screaming down the stairs. I had grabbed a robe and wrapped it around me, and I followed, trying to make him let her go. He threw her outside, naked, tossing her clothes after her. Her mother had heard the screaming and came outside to see what the commotion was.

"'Keep your disgusting, perverted whore daughter away from my wife!' he yelled. Then, he came back in and slammed the door." She glanced up at Melody again, and a tear slipped down her cheek, leaving a crooked path as it followed the scar. "He gave me the worst beating that afternoon, breaking my arm and my hip. He had pulled out a knife and stabbed me in the side, and he had just slashed me across my face when the door banged open.

"He turned around then. At first, I didn't care who it was. I was just glad to have Lee's attention diverted from me. But it was Clifford. He had heard me screaming and demanded that Lee leave me alone. That was all I heard, though, as I fell unconscious after that.

"Doc Roberts worked valiantly on me to stop the bleeding. Once he got that under control, he started resetting my bones. Mind you," she looked at Melody, "I wasn't aware of any of this. I didn't regain consciousness for three days." Melody, in spite of the horror she had felt concerning Cordelia's earlier confession,

had tears streaming down her face. Cordelia looked back into the fire. The flames were dying down now, but the embers still glowed brightly.

"When I finally came to, Doc Roberts told me of my condition. He said that the wound in my side was superficial, but I would have a permanent scar across my face. He didn't expect me to ever walk again. But he said that the baby seemed fine." She looked back at Melody, whose face was once again displaying shock. "I never knew before that day that I was with child.

"Clifford visited me and let me know that Lee would not bother me anymore. I cautiously asked him about Jessie, more concerned about her than about my husband, and he informed me that her family had quickly moved away in shame. I felt ashamed, as well, but Clifford," she paused, "well, he seemed nervous or uncomfortable, but I did not get the impression that he was judging me harshly. He's been kind to me ever since then."

"Land sakes, Cordelia!" Melody whispered, "I'm so sorry. How horrible." Looking for the silver lining, as she often did, she continued. "But look at you. You're walking now."

Cordelia wiped away a tear, but she nodded and smiled, and punctuated it with a couple of taps of her cane on the floor.

"What about the baby?" Melody asked.

"My little boy," Cordelia said, her face now competing in radiance with the embers in the fireplace. "I named him Jesse. After he was born, I asked my parents to care for him while I got my life in order. They live down in Denver City. I'm going to bring him here this summer."

Melody smiled, letting her gaze linger on Cordelia's face.

"Why didn't you tell me you have a son?" Cordelia looked at Melody, the shame returning to her face.

"I wasn't sure how to tell you without revealing everything else, which I wasn't ready to do yet." She looked timorously at Melody. "I'm sorry to shock you as I did. I hope I haven't lost your friendship."

"Oh Cordelia, no, of course you haven't." Melody paused. "I admit that I was . . . startled to find that you – well, you know." Cordelia nodded again. "But I put the blame on Lee. If he hadn't

treated you so badly, you would not have had to seek love elsewhere."

Cordelia smiled gratefully, and her eyes clouded with tears again.

§

Melody kicked plumes of powdery snow ahead of her as she walked alone through the forest, dwarfed by the pines and the tall, white-trunked, and now bare, poplars she had learned are called aspens. She had a lot on her mind. Actually, there were just two things, Clifford and Cordelia, but together, they occupied a great deal of space.

She mulled over the last few months she had spent getting to know Clifford. She had never known a kinder man than Clifford Griffin. Always a gentleman to her, and always thoughtful about his employees. Even his continued obsession – though Melody hesitated to use the word – over his dead fiancée could be seen as an expression of his deep and enduring thoughtfulness.

But it was also a little disconcerting when he decided that he had to leave, whether Melody was working or not, so he could climb the trail to the cliff where he played his violin every evening for the object of his obsession. It's true that he played the Mountain Melody nearly every evening now, sometimes with variations as he experimented with the melody. But aside from that, virtually his entire program each night consisted of melancholy classical pieces. The Mountain Melody was a tiny island of happiness surrounded by a vast sea of tears.

Melody had become quite fond of Clifford. But, even though he had tentatively resumed pursuing her, it seemed almost as if it was reluctantly, against his better judgment, and Melody was beginning to doubt the likelihood of a happy union resulting from their acquaintance.

The other part of the problem, she knew, was herself. She felt affection for Clifford, but nothing deeper than that. She couldn't determine how much of that was because of his preoccupation with his dead fiancée.

Then, there was the situation concerning Cordelia. It had taken Melody forever to fall asleep last night after hearing Cordelia's tale. Her severe mistreatment by her husband was distressing. But even more disquieting to Melody, with her stern, respectable upbringing, was the knowledge that Cordelia had engaged in unclean behavior with another woman.

Such things were just not accepted, at least not without some keen circumlocution. She had heard of two women back east, spoken of in hushed tones, who were involved in what was known as a 'Boston marriage.' It was said, publicly, that the women were simply friends, though it was presumed that, in the privacy of their home, their relationship was of a deeper, more depraved nature.

As she thought about Cordelia being in such a relationship, Melody had to admit that she felt a certain amount of satisfaction in the knowledge that her friend had found happiness during such a difficult time, regardless of who it was with. Her husband had been so horrible, her home life less than agreeable, and it was understandable that she would seek love from someone else. Jessie was nearby, and also lacking the love and warmth she needed.

Still, having been raised as a Christian, Melody was bewildered about her feelings concerning the way Cordelia went about satisfying her needs.

Even more disconcerting, though, was that unsteady sensation she was feeling again in her stomach, and with it, the knowledge that it was Cordelia who was the cause of it, and not Clifford.

12

Melody managed to avoid Cordelia the rest of the day until she and Harmony made their way to the Grizzly Bar.

During the previous months, Griz had, reluctantly, added more chairs to the side of the bar where the piano was located, as Melody and Harmony's popularity spread throughout the area. Despite his remark to Griffin a few months back about not wanting to operate a concert hall, he found that the sisters definitely attracted an audience. He insisted that those who came to occupy a seat buy at least one drink, but to his relief, he found that most of them, during the course of the evening, purchased more than one. He altered his inventory a bit, though, as many who came to hear the sisters play, particularly the women, preferred wine over beer or whiskey.

Melody and Harmony had taken it as a matter of course, but this evening, Melody's mind was preoccupied. Every love song she played was distracting to her. When they did We Sat Beneath the Maple on the Hill, *Geneva became Cordelia. As they performed* Goodbye Liza Jane, *Liza Jane became Cordelia.*

She drank three whiskeys during the course of that evening, much to Griz' dismay.

She and Harmony walked home quietly that night, as they did most nights, listening to Griffin's melancholy concert wafting down from the sky. But when they got back to the boarding house, Melody told Cordelia that she was tired and went up to her room with Harmony.

The next morning, Melody was deliberately late for breakfast and, as everyone else was lingering at the table, she went into the kitchen and nibbled on whatever was available. From there, she went directly out to wander in the forest alone, lost in her thoughts.

This became her habit for the next several months. Even as winter came and the snow covered the ground, Melody went out to walk alone in the forest. The only variation to her solitary routine would be when Griffin called on her. Some evenings, he took her out to dinner, but during those times that she spent with him, she noticed that the dizzy feeling in her stomach never reappeared. Not for him, anyway.

She remembered when she first met him, after nearly having her nose broken by the door of the Grizzly Bar. He had been so accommodating, and his kindness had appealed to her. But, sadly, nothing more had ever developed.

It could have been his insistence on attempting to keep his dead fiancée alive, the knowledge that she was ever present in his mind, as the primary audience of his nightly concert. Or, it could have been Melody's persistent and recalcitrant attraction to Cordelia. Likely, it was a combination of both.

To her despair, the less interest she felt for Griffin, the more ardently he seemed to feel for her. By the end of March, he even began speaking of love or, at least, hinting at it. He still loved Olivia, of course, and still spoke of her on occasion, and of the guilt he sometimes felt because of his new romantic interest, but Melody seemed to be becoming more central in his mind and heart. But the more attention Griffin heaped on Melody, the more Cordelia occupied the central position in Melody's heart.

Some days it was harder to avoid Cordelia. But to her credit, Cordelia never tried to force contact. Melody felt bad about it, though. She cared immensely for her. She had been Melody's best friend for months, someone she loved spending time with. Now, Cordelia had changed, at least in Melody's mind, and Melody felt uncomfortable being near her.

She found a couple of spots in the forest that became uniquely her locations to sit and think. One was a small cave near the edge of town. It wasn't very deep so there was no danger of being taken by surprise by a wild animal taking refuge deeper in, and there was a natural rocky seat for her inside the mouth of the cave. Her other favorite place was a fallen tree. Supported on one side by the stump of another long dead tree, it provided a comfortable place for her to sit, even in the snow.

Since being removed from the influence of their devout parents, both sisters had gotten out of the habit of praying. But recently, Taylor Tuttle had moved from Georgetown to Silver Plume, so that he could be closer to Harmony, and with all the time that she had been spending with him, a devout Lutheran, Harmony had taken up praying again.

Melody tried on numerous occasions to speak to God about her dilemma. She didn't know whether God was ignoring her, or if her mind was just too tightly focused on Cordelia. Whichever was the case, she never felt any relief.

On several occasions, she would spend the entire day alone, crying in the forest, begging God to help her resist the immoral temptations plaguing her. And every time, without fail, she made her way back to the boarding house still burdened with her sinful enticements.

Interestingly, though, as God paid less attention to Melody, she found that her fear of eternal punishment in hell gradually began to dwindle.

One midmorning in April, as the snow melted and green began to push through the brown, she emerged from the forest, having made an uneasy decision.

§

"Cordelia," Melody said nervously, "I need to talk to you." She spoke softly, not wishing to be overheard by anybody else in the house. She knew Harmony was upstairs in their room, getting ready to go to work at the Grizzly Bar, but she could come down at any time.

"Of course," Cordelia replied quietly, taking her cues from Melody. They went to the parlor, the room with the greatest distance from any of the bedrooms. Melody sat down in what had been her usual spot on the settee, with Cordelia in hers on the other end. Melody was a little surprised at how long it took for the words to come out, considering all the thinking and agonizing on the subject she had done in the forest, and elsewhere, over the past several months.

"Alright," she finally started with a huff, "I've been thinking a lot about what you told me that night last summer." Cordelia, her head down as she listened, nodded. "I was ready to be filled with righteous indignation over your unclean and immoral behavior. At the same time, I was willing to excuse it because of the circumstances at the time.

"I've also thought a lot about Clifford. However," Melody paused, tears accumulating in her eyes, "I've come to understand that a certain fluttering feeling in my stomach that I had been attributing to Clifford . . ." she looked at Cordelia, "this feeling was actually about you." At that, Cordelia raised her head and looked at Melody, her eyebrows drawn together.

"And I started remembering all the times you've touched me or embraced me, the times I've found you looking at me or smiling at me. At those times, I simply thought of them as evidences of your warm and friendly nature. And while you are, indeed, warm and friendly, I have not noticed those attentions being given to anyone else.

"I began to wonder if, perhaps, the sort of feelings you once felt for Jessie you might now have transferred to me." Cordelia just looked at Melody, her usual confident nature replaced by apprehension. "And I became afraid," Melody plunged onward, "that this was, in fact, what was happening, because that would mean that my improper feelings for you would be returned."

"Your feelings for me?" Cordelia asked, her voice carrying a hopeful note. "Would that be so bad?" Melody took a few breaths as she looked at Cordelia, thinking about her response.

"I don't know." She brushed the tears from her eyes. "I know I don't want to be consigned to everlasting punishment for my sins, although God doesn't seem to be paying attention to me anymore. At the same time, though," she placed her hand on Cordelia's, "I can't imagine that punishment being worse than – than being in love with you and not having my love returned."

Cordelia's lip quivered and the tears gushed from her eyes as she took Melody's hands and pressed them to her lips. Almost as quickly, though, she let them go.

"We must be careful," she said, roughly wiping the tears away. "People still remember my past transgression. Some seem to have forgiven me, likely because I haven't been involved in any similar iniquities since then, and probably because I received my just deserts. But if we were to be perceived as a couple, their tolerance, I think, would reach its end. And they would include you in their castigations. I don't want our love to cause you suffering."

They heard Harmony's footsteps coming down the stairs, and a glance at the clock on the mantel showed that it was time for them to leave.

"The only suffering I will experience," Melody said quickly, quietly, "is waiting until I can see you again tonight!"

"Land sakes!" Cordelia said, and they both smiled.

13

"Hey," Suzy said as they pulled away from the B&B, "turn left here."

"What's the matter? Are you getting cold feet about the hike?" Fin asked.

"No, I just want to see something."

Fin turned, driving slowly on the narrow gravel road. Suzy leaned forward, watching carefully out the left side, but she sat back disappointed.

"It's not there," she said. Fin stopped the car.

"What's not there?"

"The Grizzly Bar. Melody and Harmony didn't have to walk far to get there. It would have been right about here." She pointed to a cute but run-down little house, next to some sort of small building that was leaning a little to the right, its windows boarded up and every last vestige of paint stripped from its grey boards.

"You know, I so envy that ability of yours," Fin said. "You're a real life time traveler."

"I wouldn't go that far. I'm always rooted right here in my time and place."

"Yes, but for a while, it's like you become someone else. Your consciousness enters another person. You see what they see, feel what they feel. You're like Dr. Sam Beckett in *Quantum Leap*!"

"Yeah, except he could influence changes in the timeline. All I can do is watch and experience."

"Still, actually watching things happen instead of just seeing a still shot of it in a cracked and faded photograph!"

"It *is* pretty cool," Suzy agreed. "Sometimes. But, you know, you could have this ability, too."

"What are you talking about? I thought it was something you were born with."

"No," Suzy shook her head. "I didn't have this ability until about a year and a half ago."

"You *discovered* you had the ability then. But isn't it an ability that you have to already possess before you can develop it?"

"According to Lilith, and others I've spoken to, we're all essentially born with an innate connection to what we often think of as supernatural. It's just a matter of how open you are to it. Unfortunately, most people in our modern, enlightened world tend to shun that as we grow older, thinking of it as silly, naïve superstition. Which is why it's referred to as supernatural."

"The works of the devil," Fin interjected.

"Yeah, or at least fantasy." Suzy looked at Fin for a moment. One thing she appreciated about him was the close attention he gave her whenever she spoke, looking squarely at her. She tried not to get sidetracked, though. "But the more open-minded and accepting you are, the greater the chance of being able to develop those abilities.

"A skeptic wouldn't be able to make contact with a spirit, for instance. That's not to say he could never *see* a spirit, but if he did, he would likely just try to come up with some kind of scientific explanation for it. But he certainly wouldn't be open to communication with a dead person."

"Well, I'm certainly not a skeptic anymore."

"No, you're not," Suzy agreed, pondering his face again, "but you're not entirely accepting of it, either."

"That's true. I'm still kind of creeped out by it. Especially when one of them tries to kill me." Fin started the car again. "I'm just jazzed that you knew what *Quantum Leap* was without me having to tell you."

"You're not the only geek in this car. Someday I'll tell you about my Wonder Woman costume." She looked nonchalantly out her window, away from Fin.

"Your – huh?" Fin burbled, looking at Suzy and trying not to drool.

"I wonder how much Dolores knows about Cordelia," Suzy said, her thoughts now back in the past.

"You mean does she know her great-grandmother was a lesbian?" Fin asked, making a mental note to come back to the Wonder Woman costume. He put the car in gear and, knowing he'd never be able to make a U turn in these narrow roads, decided to go around the block.

"Yeah. That would have been a hard time to be gay."

"Not that it's necessarily a walk in the park now," Fin added.

"True. Even with Pride Festivals across the country and around the world, there's still so much intolerance."

Fin found Silver Street and turned toward the north. The street, unpaved like all the rest, rose at a drastic angle up the side of the mountain.

"I have a couple of gay friends," Suzy continued. "I knew them when they came out, so I had a sense of how difficult it was for them, even nowadays. For some people, it takes years. Melody had the luxury of having a lot of time on her hands. Spending months alone pondering it must have helped. But still, a hundred and thirty years ago, with the lack of acceptance back then . . ." Suzy shook her head. "I can't even imagine the constant anxiety at the possibility of being found out."

"You already experienced it in your episode this morning, didn't you?" Fin asked.

"Yes, to an extent. But Melody hasn't come out to anybody except Cordelia. They still have to keep it a tightly-guarded secret."

The road finally widened when it came to an end, and Fin saw a sign marking the trailhead. He turned around and parked at the side near a tipple, a top-heavy wedge-shaped mining structure made of old, dark timbers. They got out of the car and Fin raised his eyebrows at Suzy.

"You ready for this?"

"Ready as I'll ever be," Suzy replied, less enthusiastically than Fin had hoped.

"We don't have to do it," Fin said conciliatorily.

"No, it's fine. I said I wanted the Colorado experience. You guys love hiking in your mountains, so let's go."

Fin smiled at her 'fine, whatever you want' tone. They each grabbed their bottles of water and started up the trail. They noticed right away that it was a fairly moderate incline.

After perhaps fifteen minutes, they arrived at the first switchback and Suzy was panting. A large sign posted there showed a map of the trail. Suzy stood there with her mouth hanging open, looking at the "You are here" point, and at all the remaining switchbacks and long stretches of trail. She estimated that they had hiked less than ten percent of the trail.

She looked at Fin, standing there in a relaxed posture, reading some of the historical information on the sign.

"You're not winded at all?" she asked.

"I told you, I hike quite a bit. And I'm accustomed to the altitude." He took a swallow of water and looked at Suzy. "Do you want to head back?"

"Not on your life, buster."

"While I appreciate your competitive nature," Fin said with a smile, "I want to emphasize that the altitude is not something you want to disregard. It's serious."

"I understand. Thank you for the warning, but I can keep going. If I get too worn out, I'll let you know."

"Fair enough." They smiled at each other and turned to look down the direction they had come. From this point, they could see Silver Plume down in the valley, nestled among the conifers and the early spring green of the aspens, and busy I-70 cutting through the middle of it.

They looked at each other and, holding hands, resumed climbing the trail. Along the way, they came across a long stretch of dead fallen trees from an avalanche decades before. They also had to cross several big, metal cables stretched across the trail, leftovers from the mining operation, along with other mining debris.

Suzy commented several times on the beautiful views. Fin nodded knowingly and found himself smiling smugly almost as if he were the one single-handedly responsible for them, or at least, the one who had discovered them just for her.

They were both winded by the time they finally reached the top.

"Oh my god," Suzy said, "can you imagine having to climb that every morning just to get to your job?"

"Yeah, and then to have to do a long day of physical labor when you get up here!" Fin shook his head. "We've gotten pretty soft."

They were enjoying the views from their high vantage point when Fin noticed something that seemed out of place. A large dark grey granite obelisk stood a few yards off the trail.

Fin negotiated the boulders toward the monument, with Suzy carefully following. The marker, standing about ten feet tall, featured a crest near the top bearing an image of a mythical gryphon. Below that were the words:

Clifford Griffin
Son of Alfred Griffin ESQ. of
Brand Hall, Shropshire, England
Born July 2, 1847
Died June 19, 1887
And in Consideration of his Own Request
Buried Near This Spot

Fin and Suzy looked at each other. Suzy managed a response, under her breath.

"Huh."

§

"When is it now in your episodes?" Fin asked as they were about halfway back down the trail. Suzy was lost in her own thoughts and took a few moments to respond.

"April of 1887."

"So Griffin has two months left." Fin looked at Suzy. "We're leaving tomorrow. Can you skip ahead to see how the story turns out?"

"I don't think so," Suzy shook her head. "The episodes come as fast or as slow as they come." Fin noticed she was panting pretty hard.

"Why don't we take a rest?" He saw a large rock off the path, sheltered by some shade and he sat down on one side of it. Suzy nodded and followed him, settling herself on the other side. They each took a long drink of water and caught their breath.

"Okay," Fin said, "I can't believe I'm about to say this, considering I usually want to just rip your clothes off and make love to you." Suzy wiggled her eyebrows seductively. "Stop it. I need to think." He deliberately looked away from Suzy, smiling. "Anyway, after we get back to the B&B, why don't we hole up in our room so you can spend as much time as you can following up on Melody's episodes?"

"You're really hooked, aren't you?" Suzy asked with a grin.

"I love a good story, and we just got a major teaser up there!"

"It takes a lot out of me," Suzy replied. "After this hike, you're going to owe me big time!"

"You got it, babe. I'll pay you royalties if this story pans out."

They spent the next few minutes just relaxing, stretching their legs from the exertion of the hike. Fin had his head down a little as he rubbed the side of it. It was a bright, sunny day, and he was feeling another headache coming on. From that position, as he was looking at some of the tiny mountain flowers at his feet, an unusual texture caught his eye.

He leaned over and brushed away dirt, sand, and old plant matter to expose part of a chipped edge of stone. A larger rock, partially embedded in the ground, was on top of it, and he had to tug the rock to loosen its grip. He sat back up with the piece in his hand, brushing off centuries of dirt.

"An arrowhead?" Suzy asked.

"No, it's too big to be an arrowhead," Fin replied. It was nearly six inches long. "Probably a spearhead."

"It's beautiful."

"Yeah, it's in perfect shape. I think the Ute lived in this area, at least until we came along and ran them off." He slipped the spearhead in his pocket. "This will be a great addition to my collection."

"You have a collection?"

"A small one. Just a few arrowheads I've found on my hikes. I love history."

"So you've said," Suzy smiled. She took another sip of water and stood up. "Well, I suppose we better get back if I'm going to find out how this story ends."

14

Partly to keep up appearances, and partly because he was a genuinely nice man, Melody agreed to see Griffin when he called on a lovely Sunday afternoon. Clouds were forming in the west, but for now, it was sunny and pleasant. They meandered through town as Griffin expounded on his feelings for Melody.

"My dear, I feel I must make you understand the depth of my regard for you," he said as they wandered near the western edge of town. Melody thought that he seemed to notice her lack of feeling. He reached into the inner pocket of his coat. "For this reason, I have written down my Mountain Melody into musical notation so that you might play it on the piano, if you like. I've shared the composition with the town in general, from my perch up above, but I want to share it particularly with you. I feel it's about time I make known my lo– " he hesitated only briefly, but Melody noticed it, "my fondness for you in the language we both understand."

He handed her the item he pulled from his pocket. It was an envelope rolled and tied with a ribbon.

"This is unusual," Melody said, curiously examining the rolled envelope, and delaying facing the issue of Griffin's feelings for her. "What is it?"

"Oh, the envelope? It's oil silk. The Pony Express used to use it to protect the letters. I use it in the mine sometimes, when I need to protect plans and diagrams." He spoke quickly, as if he was anxious for Melody to open the envelope.

Inside were two sheets of paper, with the handwritten musical notations. Melody stared at the papers for a few moments, feeling a gloom settling over her, knowing that she couldn't lead him on any longer.

"Clifford," she finally said, "this is so generous of you, and I am profoundly touched by your fondness for me, and by your kind gift." She took a deep breath, her heart heavy in her chest. "But I feel I must let you know that my heart belongs to someone else."

Griffin paused and Melody turned to look at him. The hurt on his face was what she had dreaded seeing.

"Who is he?" Griffin asked. "Is it someone I know?"

"It is someone you know," Melody replied carefully, "but we're not ready to tell anyone yet."

"Of course," Griffin said, nodding and attempting a smile. "Well, having experienced such an affinity myself, I shall not attempt to come between two people in love." His lip quivered as he uttered a sigh. "But I wish you both good luck and happiness."

"Thank you, Clifford. That's so very kind of you." She held the music out to him, but he refused it.

"No, I will not take back my gift. That is for you to keep, my dear." He glanced around, as if he were self-conscious at being the center of attention, even though they were alone. "I feel rather embarrassed, now. May I escort you back?"

"I don't think so," Melody replied softly. "I think I'd like to be alone for a bit."

"Of course," he nodded. "Well, if you're sure, then I shall leave you."

"I truly am sorry, Clifford," Melody said, her eyes misting as he turned and walked back toward town.

Melody looked down at the oil silk envelope in her hand, and she sighed. A drop of water splattered on the envelope, then rolled off. The clouds that had been gathering in the west when they began their walk were overhead now, and rain drops were beginning to fall.

She remembered the cave that she took refuge in sometimes, to sit alone and think. It wasn't deep, but it was deep enough to provide shelter from the rain, and it was nearby.

She approached the rock wall of the mountain, pushed aside the brush that was growing near the entrance and went inside. As she sat on the stone outcropping that was the perfect size and shape to provide a relatively comfortable seat for her, she looked at the music. It really was a beautiful melody, sweet and happy. "Much like yourself," Griffin had said.

Melody sighed and put the papers back into the envelope, rolled it up and slipped the ribbon back around it. She put her head back against the stone wall and allowed the tears to come, as the rain pattered down on the ground outside.

§

Lulled by the rain, Melody had dozed off for a bit. When she opened her eyes, she felt a little better. A good cry and a little rest put everything in perspective.

It had been a difficult thing for her to break it off with Griffin. She didn't like hurting anybody, and Griffin was such a sweet and kind person that it only added to her pain. But while she knew that it was much more painful for him, at least she knew that she had freed him to find somebody who might return his feelings.

Hopefully somebody who was alive.

As her eyes focused from her brief nap, she saw a ridge about three feet away from her, on the opposite wall of the cave. It was as if a slight fault long ago had shifted. The upper part of the cave had slipped away and down, leaving a rough wedge-shaped shelf.

Melody looked at the oil silk envelope in her hand. Though the song was 'sweet and happy,' playing it would only make her sad, reminding her of this day when she broke Griffin's heart. She knew she would never play it.

She moved closer to the shelf and tilted her head to the side to look over it, to make sure there were no snakes or other unwelcome tenants. Then, she placed the rolled envelope on the shelf and sat back down. She couldn't see it at all. The rough lip of the shelf and the downward slant hid it from view.

She felt better about that. 'Out of sight, out of mind.'

Sighing, she looked out past the brush at the mouth of the cave and saw patches of sunlight dappling the ground. It was time to get back home.

Back to Cordelia.

§

They walked east, away from Melody's memories of Griffin a few days before. They walked slowly, Cordelia setting the pace. A few people smiled and greeted them. Some ignored them. A couple of them sneered as they walked by.

Melody was always friendly but, though nothing had been said about her and Cordelia being anything more than friends, some, apparently, considered Melody guilty by association. Melody found their judgment difficult to endure.

"How do you do that?" she asked Cordelia.

"What?"

"Act as if nothing's wrong?"

"Nothing is *wrong." Cordelia seemed confused.*

"They're looking at you as if you're a monster."

"Only a few are unforgiving," Cordelia smiled. "Most are friendly, or at least tolerant."

"Land sakes," Melody said, "I marvel at your magnanimous nature."

"Oh pish," Cordelia replied with a roll of her eyes, but she smiled at Melody appreciatively.

They passed the last house before the forest took over, and they continued into the trees.

"I never knew you enjoyed walking in the woods, too," Melody said.

"Oh, it's lovely," Cordelia replied. "And sometimes, it's the only true solitude I have. With tenants of different ages and circumstances, there is usually someone there at the house. I'm not able to do this as often as I'd like, but it's nice to get away when I can."

A few minutes later, they emerged from the trees near the bank of Clear Creek. The sound of the water tumbling past the rocks was soothing, and Melody could feel the indignation she had felt earlier at the disapproval of the townspeople beginning to dissipate. She looked at Cordelia, who smiled at her, and the annoyance vanished.

Cordelia held her hand out, Melody took it, and they came together. Cordelia's lips were soft, warm and welcoming. Melody had never felt this kind of enchantment with any of the male suitors she had known back in New York, and her arms spontaneously encircled Cordelia's body, holding her tightly.

Cordelia responded breathlessly, hungrily. She dropped her cane on the ground, and Melody helped support her as they slipped to the forest floor.

15

Fin sat in one of the upholstered chairs in the seating area, his computer on the little table in front of him. He glanced up at Suzy who was sitting on the bed, her back propped up against a few pillows.

Having determined that she was just about the prettiest thing he had ever seen, he decided to keep looking at her beyond just a glance. She was also the bravest woman he had ever known, having faced down the ghosts of three very malevolent and violent men, and won, sending them into the great beyond!

Her eyes were slightly open, looking toward the foot of the bed, but they were unfocused as, in her mind, she was living a scene in Melody Martin's life. Fin was still a little creeped out by her ability to see the lives of people long dead, but at the same time, he was also jealous of it. While she was in an episode, she was, as he had said that morning, essentially a time-traveler, but without the paradoxes.

Fin had driven to Georgetown a little while ago and brought back a small pizza. Suzy took a brief dinner and bathroom break at that time, and then went right back into it. She was a trooper!

Fin was almost happy to have this time to himself. The headache had developed a little more heft since their hike up the mountain, and he was glad to not have to engage his head too much in conversation. He picked up his glass and sipped some of the 21-year-old Ben Nevis he had brought from home. Around the ache, a thought had been tickling his brain. As he had discussed with Suzy earlier, he was considering writing a story based on Melody's life, as it was being revealed to her. He had even begun making some notes and working on a rough outline of the story.

But he had never written purely historical fiction before. He had become known as a fantasy and sci-fi writer. So, why not write a story about a character based on Suzy, someone who could communicate with the dead and see their lives. Maybe she could have a nerdy but lovable sidekick as a romantic element.

Melody's story would still be told, but as a secondary storyline.

He would have to see what Suzy thought of it. While he would likely take liberties with the story in fictionalizing it, it would still be at least party biographical.

The names have been changed to protect the innocent.

Smiling, he set his glass down and began adding some notes.

16

"Are you certain you've never had feelings for another woman?" Cordelia asked a little breathlessly, a sly smile playing about her lips. She and Melody were lying in Cordelia's bed, their faces inches apart, their arms still wrapped around each other's naked bodies. Taking advantage of an empty house, Melody had slipped into Cordelia's quarters behind the kitchen.

"Only my mother and my sister," Melody replied, also out of breath, "although in truth, I must admit that my feelings for them have always been of quite a different nature."

"Considering your indecent actions with me just moments ago," Cordelia replied with an exhausted tone, and a smile, "one would certainly hope so."

"Why do you ask?" Melody inquired, trying to ignore the reference to her immorality.

"Because you seem rather adept at pleasing a woman."

"It's a talent I've cultivated only in the last few weeks."

"I think it's accurate to say that it's a talent you've perfected, my dear."

Melody smiled in response, though her face reflected a darker mood. Cordelia noted the expression.

"What's wrong?" she asked.

Melody looked at her for a few moments. Finally, she sighed.

"I'm having a difficult time reconciling a happy life in your arms with a happy afterlife in heaven."

"Do you really think that God will punish you in hellfire for finding happiness?"

"My happiness is not the issue, but my morality."

Cordelia shifted, settling in a more comfortable position, facing Melody directly.

"I remember something interesting that Jessie told me," she said. "Her family were devout Methodists. She spent a few days reading through the entire New Testament. Did you know that Jesus never once condemned people like us?"

Melody looked at her, her eyebrows knitted together as she considered this new thought.

"I remember being taught about all these horrible things that the heathens practiced," she said, "including men being unclean with each other. I assume that applied to women, as well."

"The Apostle Paul criticized 'them that defile themselves with mankind,' which, in my opinion, is a little obscure, but he's also the one who said that women should remain silent."

Melody pondered for a moment, thinking of all the 'abominations' she remembered being taught about.

"But the Bible also talked about 'vile affections' of women who change their natural use into that which is against nature."

"Also Paul. Really, the Apostle Paul was the only one in the New Testament who had anything to say about it. He was quite verbose about a lot *of things that he considered vile and repugnant, but Jesus Christ never said a word about it."*

Melody snuggled closer to Cordelia and they passed a few quiet moments in each other's arms, their legs tangled together under the cover. Finally, Melody sighed.

"I like your interpretation," she said. "I hope it's true, because I would have quite a difficult decision to make now."

"Well, it's not my *interpretation, but Jessie's. However, I must admit that it has proven to be a comfort to me in these last few years."*

"That's the problem with a diminishing faith," Melody admitted. "You don't know for certain until you die."

"I suppose you may be right about that," Cordelia said thoughtfully. "I must admit I've never been a very 'faithful' type."

"My parents were devout," Melody said. "Their spiritual instruction seemed to take root and flourish in Harmony. With me, it just seemed to cause fear and foreboding concerning my future prospects. Which now, I find, have increased greatly."

"You're one of the sweetest, kindest people I've ever known," Cordelia said, affectionately brushing the hair out of her face. "I can't imagine that your future prospects can be too dire."

Melody gazed into Cordelia's eyes for several moments, recognizing the apparently uncharted limits of her love and kindness. She sighed, then kissed Cordelia softly, holding her tightly. They lay quietly until they heard the front door open and close. With a frantic look at each other, Melody jumped out of bed and began desperately pulling her clothes on. Cordelia laughed softly, but she got out of bed and helped Melody with the more unwieldy pieces, pulling her own clothes on afterward.

"It's just as well," Cordelia said. "I need to start supper." They kissed each other quickly, and Cordelia pushed Melody out her back door, then limped toward the kitchen.

§

"Where've you been?"

Melody jumped at the voice. She had been straightening her clothing as she walked around the house, and didn't expect to see anyone, especially not her sister. Taylor Tuttle was at her side.

"Land sakes, Harmony," she said breathlessly, "you startled me. Why, I was just out for a walk."

Harmony looked back in the direction that Melody had come. "You went for a walk in Cordelia's fenced-in back yard?"

"I meant to say," Melody replied, trying not to stammer, "I was just going *for a walk."*

"I've never known you to leave the house in such a state, even if it was only for a solitary walk." Harmony looked Melody up and down. "Your hair is disheveled, your face is flushed, and your blouse is misbuttoned."

Melody looked down at her blouse, which caused her face to flush even more.

"Melody," Harmony said with an ominous tone as she looked again toward the back of the house, "you – you haven't –" She stopped and took a deep breath. "I've heard talk around town about Cordelia. That she's an unclean and immoral woman. I hope you haven't –" She couldn't seem to bring herself to complete the question.

"Land sakes, Harmony," Melody said, exasperated, "Cordelia's a good friend. She has treated both of us very well. She doesn't deserve to be slandered so horrifically."

"Unless she truly is guilty of the things folks are saying about her," Tuttle said. "Back in the days of the sons of Israel, anyone practicing such things were to be dragged outside and stoned to death."

"Well I, for one, am very glad we are not living in the days of the sons of Israel. Taylor Tuttle, where is your Christian mercy?"

"It's not my law, Miss Melody. It's God's."

"Are you without sin, Taylor? Are you going to cast the first stone?"

"I'm not casting any stones," Tuttle replied. "I'm just telling you God's feeling on the matter."

"Meanwhile," Harmony said, "you still haven't answered my question about you and Cordelia."

"I never heard a question," Melody fired back. "You couldn't seem to get it past your lips."

"Are you and Cordelia involved in unclean and sinful relations?" Her voice was low, but there was a fire in her eyes.

Melody looked at Harmony, willing herself to tell the truth, to just come out with it and admit to her sister that she was in love with Cordelia, that her feelings for Cordelia went deeper than any she had ever experienced in her life. But she knew she couldn't. She knew that such an admission would be a life sentence for both herself and Cordelia, or a death sentence if God had his way.

But her hesitation said what she couldn't.

She noted the disgust on Tuttle's face. After her most recent exchange with him, that didn't bother her much.

What burned itself much more deeply into her heart was the expression on Harmony's face. Melody couldn't tell how much of it was horror and how much was sadness.

17

"She's your sister," Cordelia said gingerly. "Are you sure you're in agreement with her decision?"

"Well, no," Melody countered, "I'm not in agreement at all. Nor am I happy about it. But I respect her wishes."

"And you're certain you don't want to end our liaison in order to keep peace in your family?"

"Cordelia," Melody said, placing her hands on Cordelia's cheeks, "I love my sister, and I would do anything in my power to hold on to our relationship. But I would never ask her to give up something that makes her truly happy, and I resent the fact that she expects that of me.

"I love you. You *make* me *truly happy, and I know you would never ask something like that of me." Cordelia shook her head. "As much as I love Harmony, it appears I love you more."*

Cordelia's eyes filled with tears, and they clasped each other in their arms.

"Still," Cordelia said, her face buried in Melody's auburn hair, "to not be invited to your own sister's wedding. That's just so small-minded." Melody pulled away and looked at her.

"I think it was small-minded of her to move out of here, too."

"Well, she wasn't the only one."

"I know," Melody replied, looking down in shame. "Mr. Webb and Mr. Parker are the only ones left here."

"And you."

"And me." Melody looked back up at Cordelia and smiled, but it quickly faded. "I'm so sorry I brought this on you."

"Oh, Melody, you didn't bring this on me. People already knew about me from before. It's just that they have short memories."

"But I reminded them."

"If you hadn't, I probably would have said or done something that would have reminded them. I'm rather fond of you myself, and I don't know how well I can hide that.

"But that's exactly what we have to do. From now on, we have to be extremely careful. We can't express our affection in front of anyone. We can't do or say anything that reminds them that we're

depraved women, abominations. You're my friend, my companion, you assist me in running the boarding house, just helping me out because of my weaknesses. But as far as anyone else is concerned, we're nothing more. In time, they'll forget again and things will calm down."

"I hope you're right," Melody said, tightly clasping Cordelia's hands in her own.

"I know I'm right," Cordelia smiled encouragingly. "We'll be able to live out our lives, happily together, as long as we keep it quiet, and away from prying eyes."

Melody sighed as they leaned together, resting their heads on each other's shoulders. She wished she could be as confident.

18

Weary and stiff, Suzy came out of her long series of episodes yawning and stretching. The dizziness and fatigue were profound, and it took her a little while to be able to focus on her surroundings. By this time, it was dark outside and Fin had slipped under the covers next to her and was reading.

"Hey, baby," he said, "welcome back." Suzy sighed and let herself slip sideways on the headboard until her head was resting on his shoulder.

"Thanks," she whimpered.

"Are you finished?"

"For tonight. I just can't do anymore."

"That's okay, sweetheart. Do you want to talk about what you saw, or do you want to go to sleep?"

"I want to go to sleep," Suzy replied somberly, wiping the tears from her eyes, "but I don't know if I can. I'm too sad."

She spent the next several minutes telling Fin what she had witnessed. By the time she finished, with Fin's arms around her, she fell asleep with her head resting on his chest.

§

"Melody, I can't tell you how sorry I am about your sister's reaction to your news," Suzy said as Melody greeted her in her sleep.

Melody smiled sadly.

"Thank you. But what about you?" Melody looked at her with her eyebrows drawn together. "Don't you think ill of me for this revelation?"

"No, Melody, of course not. Times have changed. A little bit, anyway. There are still some religious fundamentalists who feel that being gay is an unforgivable sin, but many of us are learning that it's something a person is born with, the way they're made, not just a sinful alternative lifestyle."

She didn't know how much of that terminology was familiar to someone from the nineteenth century, but Melody seemed to grasp her meaning.

"Thank you, Suzy," she said. She made a motion of wiping away tears, as had other spirits Suzy had interacted with, despite the lack of such physical accouterments as tear ducts.

"And I'm sorry I couldn't finish your story tonight. I'm just so tired. This takes a lot out of me."

"That's alright," Melody smiled. "I'm just happy to know you appreciate my story."

"I do, so much. We're leaving tomorrow, but maybe I can see another chapter tomorrow morning before we leave." She didn't know if Melody would know the word 'episode.'

"Land sakes, that's splendid!" Melody said, clasping her hands together, apparently her bubbly self again. "I'll send you off with a happy ending."

"You're so sweet," Suzy said. "It's been such a pleasure getting to know you."

§

Once again, she awoke early, while Fin was still asleep, and she quietly got out of bed. She settled herself in the chair that Fin had occupied the previous evening.

She placed her palms upward on the table. Still lacking a candle, she closed her eyes and began her meditation routine, picturing a candle in her mind.

17

Melody sighed as the forest enveloped her. The foliage around her blurred as her eyes filled with tears. It was a warm day and the green shade was welcome. Besides, she had been spending so much time outdoors that she was beginning to turn brown. Harmony had told her, back when she was still speaking to her, that soon she was going to look like a farm hand.

Despite her bold statements to Cordelia, Harmony's rejection did bother her a great deal. From childhood, she and her sister had been inseparable. True, they were different in many ways, but they had always been supportive of each other, filling in whatever quality the other lacked. They had been as close as if they were twins.

Melody felt a great void now.

She found her fallen tree and plopped herself down on it, swinging her feet under her. She brushed the tears from her eyes, but they were replaced by more.

Still, her relationship with Cordelia went a long way toward filling that void she was feeling. It was different from the familial conformity she had always experienced with Harmony, but it was so full of love.

In spite of the sorrow she was feeling, though, she couldn't help but smile whenever she thought of Cordelia. She was so kind, so loving, so agreeable that even the scar that slashed across the side of her face and her constant limp did little to dim her beauty in Melody's eyes.

Griffin had called a couple more times since Melody had cut it off with him. His continued pining over his long-dead fiancée notwithstanding, his attraction to Melody was so strong that an abrupt withdrawal seemed impossible. Melody didn't know if he had heard any of the rumors, but she had gently yet firmly let him know that there could be no relationship between them.

Having to revisit that again was difficult for Melody, as she cared about Griffin. But she loved Cordelia, and she was looking forward to spending the rest of her life with her, and to meeting Cordelia's little boy, Jesse, who was to join her next month. Together, they would be a happy, if unconventional, family.

Even if nobody else could know of their love, she and Cordelia would know, and that made Melody happy. Looking around her, blinking through her tears, the forest was still a blur, but she didn't care. She had her precious outdoor solitude, she had the sunlight filtering through the trees, and she had Cordelia. She may have had a difficult thing to deal with where her sister was concerned, but she had so much to be thankful for.

She was happy.

20

"Go straight," Suzy said as Fin drove away from the B&B. He figured that, like the day before, she wanted to see something from her episodes, so he passed the turn to get to I-70. The street didn't go very far. It turned to the left at a rickety, boarded up little house.

"Park over there," she instructed, pointing to a weed-covered area in front of the little house. She was out of the car before he had his seatbelt off.

"What's going on?" he asked as he got out.

"There used to be two other houses beyond this one," Suzy said as she trudged single-mindedly into the trees. "They must have either been torn down, or the forest reclaimed them."

Fin followed her, hoping that the reason for her impromptu hike became clear before too long. Soon after, he saw rotted wood and the remains of a stone fireplace, with trees growing through and around it. They were skirting the base of the mountain, surrounded by aspens as well as new- and old-growth pines. Suzy was constantly looking around, but seemed to know where she was going.

Finally, she came to a stop, looking at the wall of rock on her right. She started pushing at some heavy brush, and Fin came to her side and assisted, standing on some of it to get it out of the way, revealing a small indentation in the side of the mountain.

Suzy stooped and went into the little cave, sitting down on a rocky outcropping that served well as a seat. She sat there with her eyes closed for a moment, then she sighed and looked to her right. She tilted her head back, the top of her head already brushing the top of the cave.

Melody must have been several inches shorter than me, she thought.

Tilting her head, she looked over the little ledge up to her right and reached in, pulling out a strange, dusty item.

"Is that what I think it is?" Fin asked, stooping outside.

"I think so," Suzy said. "It must be."

She came out of the cave and stood up. She held what looked like a scroll, tied with a ribbon that might have once been red. She slipped the ribbon off and just the friction of sliding half the distance of the envelope was enough to break it apart. But the oil silk envelope, though yellowed and coated in dirt and cobwebs, seemed to be in reasonably good condition, considering its age.

Suzy gingerly unrolled it and opened the flap, which made a little less of a cracking sound than she had expected, and she looked inside. With tears in her eyes, she smiled and held it open for Fin, so he could see inside. There were two sheets of paper with handwritten musical notations on them.

"Mountain Melody," Fin said, reading the title written at the top of the page in, apparently, Clifford Griffin's hand.

§

Suzy didn't want to handle the old papers any more than she had to, so she left them in the envelope, holding it loosely on her lap as Fin made the drive east on I-70 back to his house. It was noon when they got back. After carrying their luggage in the house, Suzy carefully pulled the papers out of the envelope.

"For 132-year-old paper, they're in surprisingly good shape," Fin noticed.

"I know," Suzy agreed. "It's yellowed, but it doesn't seem to be terribly brittle."

"Still, why don't we make copies so we don't have to handle the originals?"

In his library a couple of minutes later, having lightened the copies a bit, Suzy slipped the originals back into the envelope.

"Now, I just wish I knew how to play an instrument," Suzy said.

"Come with me," Fin replied.

He took the copies from her and led her upstairs and into a room she hadn't been in yet. Suzy looked around at the baby grand in the corner, two guitars, an acoustic and an electric, on stands, a digital keyboard and various other instruments scattered about.

"Aren't you posh!" Suzy said. "You have a music room?"

"Well, I call it my hobby room," Fin replied. "It's not just for music."

Suzy looked around the room and saw that, interspersed among the instruments were glass cases displaying assorted collections, using them as decorative elements in the room. The displays showcased a variety of collections from *Star Wars* paraphernalia to antique teacups.

Fin sat down at the piano and put the copies of the music on the music rack in front of him.

"Really?" Suzy said. "Is there anything you *can't* do?"

"Relax," Fin said, "I didn't say I was any good."

He studied the music and picked out the tune, shakily at first. Suzy placed the envelope containing the original music on the piano as she listened to Fin getting familiar with the music. Then, the second time through, Fin was a little more comfortable and played it more confidently.

"That's it," Suzy said, clearly moved by the melody, "that's the song I heard echoing down into the valley. It's beautiful. And, by the way, you're just disgustingly talented."

Fin smiled and blushed a bit, affecting something of an 'aw shucks' posture.

"Being an introvert, I've had lots of time to myself, to cultivate creative interests of mine. It's only been in the last few years that I've been able to afford to pursue some of the ones that don't bring in any money."

He looked back at the music.

"I'm guessing about some of it," he said. "The time signature is easy enough. The song is in three-quarter time, so it's basically a waltz, but Griffin didn't note the tempo.

However, considering the subject matter and his feelings for her, and the fact that it's a waltz, I'm assuming it's *adagio* or thereabouts."

"Okay," Suzy replied with a shrug, understanding little of what he said, "whatever. It's a beautiful song." She looked at Fin. "I don't suppose you can play the violin and play it as it was originally done, from Clifford Griffin's cliff?"

"No, I'm afraid not," Fin smiled.

"Well, what good are you, then?" Suzy asked. Her smiling glance at him, and her lingering touch on his shoulder, belied her words.

She started an idle circuit of the room, as Fin played the song through for a third time, and she looked at the various collections in the glass cases. The *Star Wars* and Marvel superhero action figures didn't surprise her. Then she saw Fin's collection of Indian arrowheads.

"Oh," she said, as he finished playing, "that's right. You said you had a small collection of arrowheads."

"Oh yeah," Fin replied, "I think that spearhead is still out in the car. I'll go out and get it in a minute." He looked back at the music in front of him on the piano. "In the meantime, what do you want to do with this music?"

Suzy turned back to him and thought for a moment.

"I think Dolores should have it," she said. Fin smiled at her.

"What a nice idea. Do you want to just go there and give it to her and come back, or do you want to stay again?"

"Why don't we stay for a night or two? Melody gave me a happy send-off, but she didn't really finish her story."

21

"What was that?" Suzy asked urgently as she sat up in bed, her hand gripping Fin's shoulder.

"What was what?" Fin asked groggily.

"You didn't hear that?"

"No," Fin replied, at the exact moment that a bump sounded somewhere in his house. "Okay," he said, "that's not the usual bump in the night of a house settling."

"No, I didn't think so either."

Fin rubbed his eyes and got out of bed, opening the bedroom door. Straining his ears, he listened again. Another sound reached his ears, one that sounded like something being bumped across the hardwood floor.

He walked down the hallway and heard another bump. It came from his hobby room. Wishing he was wearing pants, he opened the door and turned on the light.

There was nobody there.

"What is it?" Suzy asked, startling Fin, as he hadn't heard her come up behind him.

"It's nothing," he replied. "There's nobody here."

"But we both heard it."

"I know," Fin said. "Maybe it *was* the house settling." He turned off the light and closed the door, and they both heard a loud thud from inside the room. Fin threw the door open and turned on the light again, and again, nobody was there.

But the piano bench was lying knocked over on its back.

"What the hell?" Fin said as he walked toward the piano. He righted the bench, and he noticed the music on the piano. He looked at Suzy, his eyes narrowed.

"Can a ghost attach itself to an object?" he asked.

"What do you mean?" Suzy asked.

Fin pointed at the oil silk envelope, lying where Suzy had left it.

"I don't know," Suzy replied, as she pondered the envelope. "You think Melody came back with us?"

Fin shrugged and looked back at the music.

"It's the only thing I can think of. She's not familiar with my house and she's knocking things over."

"But spirits are non-corporeal," Suzy said, confused, "intangible. Wouldn't she just walk *through* the things she wasn't familiar with?"

"You're asking me? You know more about it than I do. But I just know I've heard of reports of ghosts disturbing people, making noises in a house, moving furniture, things like that."

"I'll contact Lilith in the morning and see what she says."

Fin nodded, and he closed the door, but he left the light on.

"I just hope we can get some sleep until then."

Suzy hoped to make contact with Melody as she fell asleep, but instead, she went into a dream that involved Fin wearing a *Ghostbusters* uniform.

§

As usual, Suzy woke up early. Slipping quietly out of bed, she went downstairs and into the kitchen where she started making a cup of tea. She had to settle with heating a cup of water in the microwave since Fin didn't have a teapot or kettle.

If this relationship is going to work . . . she mused.

As the teabag steeped, Suzy sat on the stool where she had watched him make French toast a few days before. She fondly remembered his easy way in front of the stove, his comfortably casual posture as he talked to her, and she smiled.

But she had other business to attend to now. She placed her hands on the counter, palms facing up, and she closed her eyes.

She sought that ripply sensation, the strange, uneasy feeling that usually preceded the beginning of an episode. But there was nothing. She stayed solidly rooted in the present, in Fin's modern kitchen.

She looked at the clock on the microwave. It would be nearly 9:00 in Marblehead. She picked up her phone and scrolled through her contacts list, pressing Lilith's number.

"Hi, Lilith," she said when Lilith answered after five rings, "it's Suzy Quinn."

"Oh, hello, Suzy," came the soft, little-old-lady voice that Suzy remembered so well from her first time meeting her. Leanne, the pastor of the little Church of Spiritual Science in Marblehead had introduced them when Suzy had questions about the first ghost she had encountered in her carriage house. She had consulted her a couple of times after that when she had follow-up questions. "How are you, dear?"

"I'm fine, thanks. How are you doing?"

"Well, I can't complain." She usually sounded as if she was smiling. "What can I do for you?"

"I have a question. Can a spirit attach itself to an object and be moved from its original location?"

"Oh, yes, spirits often attach themselves to objects, whether it's something as small as a piece of jewelry or as large as a house. It could be an object that had sentimental value to them in life, or perhaps something of value to a loved one. Why do you ask?"

"I'm in Denver visiting a friend, and we spent a few days at a B&B in the mountains. I made contact with the spirit of a girl from the 1880s. Before we came back, I followed some clues and found a piece of sheet music that was written for her, and which she hid in a cave.

"Well, we got back yesterday, and last night, we heard noises in my friend's music room, as if things were being bumped or scooted around, and one time, the piano bench was knocked over."

"Oh dear. Yes, it does sound as if you may have brought that spirit back home with you. Since you called me, I assume you haven't spoken to her yet?"

"I tried, but I wasn't able to make contact. There was just nothing there."

"She may be frightened. You've taken her from the area she's been in for over a century and put her in a new and unfamiliar place."

"Okay, good to know. What about the bumping and knocking over the piano bench? I thought spirits could just walk through things."

"Well, that's true. But again, she's in an unfamiliar place. Being frightened, she's probably just, what we might call acting out. She's taking out her frustrations on whatever happens to be nearby. Try to make contact with her and calm her fears."

"Sure, but I already tried that, and I couldn't even sense her presence."

"That's not surprising. If she's afraid, she may be hiding."

"Hiding?" Suzy asked.

"Yes. Of course, as a spiritual being, she doesn't need to *physically* hidc from you, but she could be masking her presence from you. She might even feel betrayed.

"Be patient and keep trying. Be gentle. Let her know that you care and that what happened was not intentional. Once you've made contact with her, you can help her to move on to the next plane."

"Okay," Suzy said.

"I was right about you," Lilith said, a knowing, almost smug tone in her voice.

"About what?"

"That you have SpiritSense, that you're a lightworker."

"Oh, Lilith, I don't know about that," Suzy sighed.

"Well, it's not for me to say. It's only for you to prove."

"Okay," Suzy said again, anxious to slough off the praise Lilith was heaping on her. "Thank you so much, Lilith."

"It's my pleasure, dear. And good luck."

§

Suzy spent a few more minutes trying, unsuccessfully, to make contact. She didn't feel anything at first, no mood, no impression of any kind, no consciousness. If Melody was hiding from her, as Lilith suggested, she was doing a really good job! *Maybe I need to do this in Fin's hobby room.*

But then, she began to sense something, a cautious presence. It seemed as if she was perceiving it through a haze, as if from a great distance, which also seemed to support the thought of embarking on this in the hobby room, closer to the Mountain Melody sheet music.

She opened her eyes and stood up. She took a sip of her tea, then she padded back up the stairs and cautiously opened the door to Fin's music room. Or hobby room, as he seemed to prefer.

The room was pretty much as they had left it. She couldn't tell if anything had been moved slightly or not, but everything was still upright. She looked a little more closely at the room itself than she had when Fin first brought her in here. Yesterday, she had noticed the instruments, then the display cases.

This morning, she noticed the dark grey panels of foam placed on the walls. They had intriguing shapes cut into them, as if they were pieces of art, but Suzy assumed they were to dampen echoes for the sake of the music, or something like that. She also noticed that there were no windows in the room. With the light turned off, it would have been pitch black in there.

She left the light on.

She sat down on the piano bench, placing her tea on a coaster on a shelf behind her. Settling herself comfortably on the bench, her hands resting on her knees, palms up, she began another attempt to contact Melody. She closed her eyes and tried to be as open and receptive as possible.

Suzy could feel her presence, but again, it was cautious and hesitant. She could sense confusion, disorientation, even fear. She tried to project positive feelings, a sense of welcoming, but she couldn't tell if those feelings were being received.

She gave up on it when Fin came in the room.

"Any luck?" he asked.

"No," she sighed, picking up her cup of tea.

"Are you sure she's even here?"

"Yes, I can feel her presence. But she's confused and afraid. She's been in that place for a long time, and now, suddenly, she's been plopped in a different, unfamiliar, modern place, against her will. Lilith suggested that she may be hiding from me."

"I'm sorry," Fin said, affectionately brushing her cheek with his fingertips. Suzy smiled at the sympathetic tone in his voice.

"You've really come around from being creeped out by it," she said.

"Well," he replied with a hesitant tone, "I still think talking to dead people is a little creepy. And I admit I'm not thrilled about having one in my house. But like you've said, they're just people. And the way you've described Melody, she seems like a nice one. As a confirmed introvert, I can certainly sympathize with being forced to be someplace where you're uncomfortable. For me, that includes a *lot* of places."

Suzy placed her hand on his in an act of sympathy of her own.

"Why don't you start on some breakfast for us," she said, "and I'll give it another try."

"You got it," Fin said, as he leaned over and kissed her.

"Hmm," she mused to herself as she watched him walk away. She pulled herself back to the task at hand after he closed the door.

She drained the last swallow of her tea and put the cup down. She took a deep breath and closed her eyes, trying to put herself in the most relaxed and non-threatening mental state she could muster.

She could sense the presence again, though she couldn't locate it. Concentrating on that, Suzy opened her mind and heart, welcoming Melody, attempting something like a mental embrace.

I'm here, Melody. I'm your friend. You're safe here. You don't have to hide from me.

For a moment, the darkness inside her eyelids lightened a little. She didn't see an image. Rather, it was formless and cloudy, but it was green.

Encouraged, she smiled, and the state of mind that the smile engendered and reinforced seemed to reach her target audience. Cautiously, Suzy opened her eyes just a bit, and she saw Fin's hobby room start to blur, colors swirling and melding together, and it felt as if Melody was guardedly opening up to Suzy's probing.

In time, the hobby room disappeared and forest appeared around her, as she seemed to pick up where she had left off in the last episode in Silver Plume.

22

She was surrounded by green. The forest engulfed her, though again, she couldn't see details. It was blurry and dark, as if a heavy fog permeated the woods. Or perhaps she had stayed out later than she had intended. Occasionally, a shaft of light penetrated through the foliage, diminishing the gloom, and she reveled in that light. But still, it remained unclear.

In fact, everything *was unclear. Her feelings, physical sensations, sights and sounds. She couldn't understand why everything was such a blur.*

Still, she seemed to feel at home. What little she could discern about her surroundings was comforting to her.

She took a deep breath, and she smiled as she actually smelled the scent of the forest.

23

Suzy came out of the short episode smiling herself, feeling a sense of accomplishment. She sat for a moment, happy that she had made contact again. Then, she was up and moving. She had to tell Fin.

He was just starting to chop some mushrooms when Suzy came into the kitchen.

"I got her!" she said.

"That was fast!" Fin replied. "I just came down here five minutes ago."

"I know, it was a very short episode. But it was almost as if it started up right where it left off in Silver Plume. She was in the forest, just wandering alone. I couldn't see much, because it was still blurry."

"She was crying again?"

"I don't know," Suzy said, ruminating on the episode. "It didn't seem like it, but admittedly, the feelings were kind of blurry, too. If Lilith was right, it could be that Melody was still a little put out at me. She may have just been holding back her feelings a bit."

"Well, it sounds like you're starting to break through. It may just take a little time to reestablish that trusting connection with her."

"Sure. I just feel so bad making that reconnection necessary. She seemed happy where she was, and I ripped her away."

"But you didn't know. And like you said, we're going to take the music to Dolores, so we'll return Melody to her home."

§

They ate their omelets, happily discussing plans for their next trip to Silver Plume. When they were finished, Suzy helped Fin clean up the kitchen. Afterwards, Fin went into his library, to make reservations at the B&B in a few days, at the first available vacancy. Then, he spent a few minutes staring at his computer screen, reveling in the intoxicating feeling of typing the first paragraphs of a new story. While he did that, Suzy went back upstairs to try to make contact with Melody again.

24

She was walking purposefully, as if she knew exactly where she was going. Everything still looked blurred, but some feelings had returned. She heard the crunch of pine needles, leaves and twigs as she walked, and she felt moisture, perhaps early morning dew, on her bare feet. In the middle of her blurry vision, she saw a large rock ahead of her, at least as tall as she was, jutting out of the ground, surrounded on three sides by heavy forest. That's where she was going. Behind that rock, in the shelter of the forest, was their place.

Despite the determination in her walk, there was a dullness, a disorientation. She couldn't understand it. She slowed her steps as she tried to recall why she was going there. It was as if she knew where she needed to be, but couldn't remember what to do once there. It had been so long!

Suddenly, she stopped as somebody grabbed her hand from behind, pulling her around. She looked at the face, and though her view of it was unclear, blurry, she knew she recognized it, and she laughed.

She pulled her hand free and ran, but she felt hands grab onto her by the garment she was wearing. She wasn't wearing much. Ah, the freedom and privacy of the forest.

She felt a determined yank from behind her, pulling her down to the ground, and her clothing came apart. Still, she laughed, until she felt a loving hand cupping her breast. That was clear, at least, the physical sensations. She inhaled and moaned when she felt fingers grasp her nipple and squeeze lightly. Her body tensed when she felt a tongue teasing her other nipple.

As her nipple was suddenly engulfed by warm, wet lips, the hand let go of her other nipple, caressing it and spreading out from there, before slipping down lower. She felt the fingers tickle softly down her belly, savoring every curve they encountered. They stopped temporarily at the tangle of hair, fondling the strands.

As the hand moved downward, she opened her legs, welcoming the touch that she knew was coming. She felt the hand cover the hills and valleys, while one finger went exploring more closely.

It slipped over the soft ridges and into the wetness between, then started moving up, searching for the little mound.

When the finger found it, her torso went rigid, and lights flashed in her mind as if every nerve ending in her body were all firing at once.

Then, it went black.

25

"Whoa!" Suzy exclaimed as she was thrown out of the episode. She sat back against the wall, panting, holding herself up with her hands on each end of the piano bench. She felt dizzy and disoriented, which was not uncommon when exiting one of her episodes. But she felt something else, a residual something from the unfinished lovemaking in the forest.

She squeezed her legs together, trying to calm the sensation, and was only partly successful.

I need Fin!

§

Fin had been tapping happily at his computer for several minutes, but still he was pleasantly surprised by the interruption of Suzy grabbing him and engaging him in some deep kissing, straddling him on his chair.

Still fully clothed, for the moment, anyway, her grinding against him had the effect of making his jeans particularly tight. That seemed to beneficially affect the contact that Suzy felt, and she moaned.

Fin had always been told to take his time. He knew that women, in general, take longer to 'get there' than men do. They need to be romanced. He had always tried to abide by that principle, so that sex was good for both of them, not just him.

Now, Suzy seemed to be throwing that out the window. He decided to just follow her lead.

She pulled away just enough to look at his face, and when Fin saw the lustful intensity of her expression, it caused an even greater surge in the swelling he was experiencing. Suzy reached down and managed to get his jeans unfastened, and he sighed when he felt her hand feeling around inside.

He was amazed that she didn't even need any foreplay, but she slipped off his lap and pulled his pants down, taking him in her mouth. That could have lasted a lot longer than it did, as far as he was concerned, but he didn't complain when Suzy stood up and quickly stripped her clothes off and pulled his face toward her neatly trimmed pubes.

He reached up and grasped her buttocks, pulling her against him, and he probed with his tongue. The angle wasn't great from where he sat, but she tilted her hips forward a little to accommodate him. He knew it was at least a little effective when he found her clit and caressed it a few times with the tip of his tongue. He felt her body convulse and she gasped, keeping his face pressed against her.

Finally, she released him, but when he looked up at her face, the intensity was still there.

"I need you inside me!" she said breathily. She resumed her initial position, straddling him, although the effect was greatly improved by the lack of clothing between them. As he entered her, they both uttered a guttural moan. All Fin could do was sit there and watch Suzy's naked body sliding up and down on him, her breasts bouncing in an intriguing rhythm.

It only took a couple of minutes before that moment arrived. Suzy quivered a few times as Fin pulsed inside her, then she collapsed forward into his arms.

§

"So, you made contact again, huh?" Fin asked a little breathlessly, still inside her, but relaxing, as Suzy lay forward, panting against him. His fingertips were slipping up and down Suzy's body, now slick with sweat.

"Did I ever!" Suzy replied. "Melody was in the forest, and apparently Cordelia was there with her again. But I couldn't see details. It was blurry like the last time in Silver Plume, when Melody was crying."

"But she wasn't crying this time?" Suzy sat up and looked at him with some of that residual intensity from earlier.

"Not even close!"

"Thank her for me next time you see her," Fin sighed. "So, why do you think it was still blurry this time if she wasn't crying?"

"I don't know for sure. But considering what Lilith said, and how difficult it was to make contact with Melody in the first place, it could be that she's still upset about being moved, and not very open yet. If she's holding back, maybe that's affecting the quality of the visuals I'm receiving."

"Poor reception, huh? You might have to jiggle the antenna a little," Fin quipped.

"Yeah, that's what I'm trying to do."

"That was no antenna," Fin replied, raising an eyebrow at her. Suzy grinned and flushed a bit, moving her hips forward a little, to keep him inside her as long as possible.

"Anyway," she continued, "maybe she's still put out at us for taking her away from Silver Plume, and she's just not opening up to me yet."

"Well, it's a start, anyway. Maybe you'll get that back."

"I hope so. I'd still like to see how her story ends."

26

It was fairly dark inside the nest, with just a little green-tinted twilight filtering through the door opening ahead of her, and brighter orange light flickering from a fire, vented through the roof. She was busily grinding leaves on a flat rock. It was still blurry, but she could see a little more detail now. She brushed the powdered leaves into a cup-like receptacle made of bark, and dribbled a few drops of water into it, mixing it with her finger. She added more water until she was satisfied with its consistency.

She turned toward the figure lying on the ground, covered with furs but still shivering despite the warmth of the day. She held the cup to the person's mouth and tipped it until all the liquid was gone.

Now, she just had to wait.

§

The green-tinted light from outside the nest had faded to black, but the fire was still burning. She had busied herself with other activities, mixing concoctions from assorted plants and roots, some to leave here, and others to take with her when she left.

She heard a quiet sound to her side and she turned. The man who was lying there was still. He was no longer shivering, but she sensed that he was looking at her.

She said something to him, but the sound was as unclear as the visuals. The man replied, and she smiled, satisfied with the answer. The sound attracted another woman who was behind her, and she came to the man's side, the fire gleaming on her dark skin. She was followed by their small children.

The woman helped the man pull the furs off of him, and she leaned over and hugged him, placing her forehead against his. He pulled himself up on his elbow, and the young family all turned their attention to her and smiled as she began gathering up her things. The mother and father both said something to her, and she smiled back at them and nodded.

She left a couple of the concoctions with them, with instructions, and then she left. She walked through the forest, past other similar structures, and as usual, she focused her attention on the sounds of the forest, careful to allow privacy for those inside the nests.

At the edge of the little village, she came to her own nest, a structure made of skin stretched over large sticks stuck into the ground. She entered the hut and put down the things she had been carrying, breathing a sigh of relief.

There beside their own fire, she saw a familiar figure, and she smiled.

27

"You're telling me we somehow brought home a different ghost?" Fin asked, trying really hard to keep the alarm out of his voice. He sat on the grass in his front yard where he had been pulling weeds.

"Looks that way," Suzy said, her eyes narrowed as she recalled the episode. "I still couldn't see much detail, but it appeared to be some kind of Native American village, the people living in skin huts. From what I could make out, this woman seemed to be a sort of healer." She looked up at Fin. "Didn't you mention a particular tribe that used to live around Silver Plume?"

Fin looked at her for a moment before recognition flickered in his eyes.

"The spearhead?"

"That's what I'm thinking."

"So, it wasn't the music at all."

"No, which actually makes more sense when you think about it. Melody's spirit is at the B&B, not in that cave."

"Hmm," Fin nodded. "Yeah, there were several bands of Ute Indians living throughout Colorado, until the white man pushed them westward. The state of Utah was named after them." Fin sat in thought for a few moments, then he looked at Suzy. "So, you think we have the ghost of a dead Indian who's likely pissed at white people for taking their home from them?"

"Relax, princess," Suzy teased, "this one was obviously living in Silver Plume when she died. That's where her spirit was."

"True. Probably *killed* by a white man."

Suzy sighed, but it was accompanied by a smile.

"One good thing about *this* case, I guess," Fin said, "is that the ghost is not attached to my house, but to an object that can be removed. All I have to do to get rid of the ghost is to get rid of the spearhead."

"Finley MacKinley!" Suzy purposely used his full name, which she knew he didn't like. "You can't do that!"

"Why not?"

"Because that's not just some weird, impersonal force up there. She's a person. She's still here because of some kind of traumatic experience, and if you just toss the spearhead away, you're tossing her away, too."

"You're right," Fin replied. "Sorry, I was thinking only of myself." He looked at Suzy with admiration. "I wish I was as strong as you are."

"Psh," Suzy said dismissively. "I'm not so strong. I just care about people. Living or dead."

"And I'm a heartless bastard."

"No," Suzy replied, pressing his shoulder affectionately, "you're just a little newer at this than I am. And you're not the one actually experiencing it, getting to know these people."

"And the way I was raised, ghosts weren't real. Haunted houses were occupied by demons, fallen angels, not the spirits of dead people."

"Yeah, I guess religious beliefs can be tough things to recover from."

"So," Fin said, perking up a little, "what's our course of action?"

"Well, I think I owe it to this woman to learn her story, after which I'll try to help her move on." She looked at Fin with a concerned look. "I wonder if she speaks English."

28

The darkness was fading slowly. She could see a portion of the sky through the smoke vent above where she lay in their nest. As the stars flickered away and the sun slowly approached the horizon, she knew that the sunrise wasn't far off. She turned and she could barely see him lying beside her, hear him breathing. White Wolf.

The image was becoming clearer now. She could see his face as he opened his eyes and smiled at her from a short distance away. She felt a little warm, so she pushed the skin down, letting the cool morning air wake them up. He reached for her and she let him pull her closer to him. She felt the warmth of his skin against hers in the cool morning air. She felt his arousal as he pulled her body tightly against his.

She pressed her face into his neck, breathing his musky scent, and she wrapped her leg around his. Just as he pressed his lips against hers, they heard footsteps rapidly approaching their nest. There was a quick tapping upon one of the supporting branches near the entrance of their shelter, and she reluctantly pulled herself away from him. She got up and stooped through the opening and saw a man from her village standing there, his face lined with worry.

He said something to her. She heard the alarm in his voice, but the words were still unclear. Still, she got his meaning. She ducked back into her nest, grabbed a leather pouch and said something to White Wolf as he waited. He sighed and nodded at her, and he pulled the skin back up over him as she left.

Now that she was outside her nest and walking through the village, she felt chilled, and she wished she had wrapped a skin around herself before she left. But they quickly arrived at his home and she stooped through the opening.

She smelled it immediately, the close, pungent scent of illness permeating their shelter. The same she had smelled in others. She had been kept busy the last few days.

His wife lay there shivering violently under a heavy fur, and their baby lay nearby, already grey and still in the dim light of the embers of their fire pit. She choked back a sob at the sight of their dead baby.

She mixed the potion quickly, too familiar with the procedure. This woman was much sicker than the man she had treated a few nights ago, the illness much more advanced. She decided to make the concoction a little more potent. Once she was finished mixing it, she lifted the woman's head and helped her to swallow the solution.

All she could do now was wait and hope.

She said as much to the man, but before they could even settle down to wait, there came a tapping at the entrance of his nest. He went outside and she heard a tense exchange. She recognized the voice, and she followed him out.

"What's wrong?" she asked.

"Red Flower is sick," he said, to the best of her recollection. She glanced at the other man for the briefest moment before she bent down and grabbed her bag from inside the shelter. She stood back up and told the first man that she would return. Then, she followed the other man. They didn't have far to go.

Ducking in through the entrance, she saw her friend shivering under her covers. Fighting back the tears, she quickly began mixing the potion.

27

They were sitting now in the family room, a name that Fin always felt strange calling it, living here alone. With Suzy in it with him, though, it seemed like a perfectly good name for it.

"Apparently, she's something like a medicine woman or shaman," Suzy related as she caught her breath after emerging from the latest episode. "There's some kind of epidemic rampaging through her village, and she's tirelessly trying to eradicate it."

"So she's a lightworker, too," Fin said.

Suzy looked at Fin.

"I guess she is." She paused in thought. "Do you know of any deadly illnesses that swept through the Ute people around this time?"

"Nothing specific," Fin replied, "but our history with the Native Americans is rife with killing, whether by gun or by disease."

"Yeah, that's true. She's really upset by it. It seems a good friend of hers has come down with it."

"Oh, so you can actually see what's happening around you now?"

"I can, but at the beginning, I couldn't hear clearly. When somebody spoke, it was like they were mumbling. The sound was muffled, like a weird, unrecognizable drone. It was only at the end of this episode that I was finally able to sort of understand a few words."

"Strange. Have you experienced that before?"

"No, I haven't." Suzy pondered for a moment. "I suppose it could be the fact that they're speaking in a language I don't understand. But if that's the case, I don't know how I understood the last couple of sentences in this most recent episode."

"I have a theory," Fin contemplated.

"I'm listening."

He mulled it over in his mind for a few moments, getting his thoughts in order.

"You've said that when you contact these ghosts, you make a kind of psychic connection with them, that you, to an extent, feel what they feel."

"That's true."

"Maybe, during the time you're connected to that ghost, you're sort of hard-wired into their mind, so that you not only feel what they feel, but you understand what they understand."

"Interesting," Suzy replied thoughtfully.

"So your understanding of what is said isn't dependent on understanding the words, but understanding the thought, the reception of it by the person you're connected to. You get the meaning of what's said without having to actually know the language."

"You know, that actually makes a lot of sense. When did you become a ghost psychic expert?"

"Oh, you know, I've just had a lot of time to think about things while you've been dwelling in the past with your Old Ones." He made a point of adding a whimper to his voice and trying to look dejected and brokenhearted.

"Aw, poor baby," Suzy replied sarcastically, patting his hand. But then, her face seemed to display a measure of guilt about his comment. "I haven't exactly spent a lot of time with you on this trip, have I?"

"Hey, it's not the quantity but the quality. I think I'm still glowing from our last quality time together." He grinned and took her hand in his, and as they gazed into each other's eyes, the grin turned into a smile full of warmth.

It was at that moment that Fin realized that he was actually falling in love with Suzy. Despite his flippant remark, he became aware of the fact that their lovemaking was more than just sex.

Suzy sighed as she saw the change on his face. She was surprised that she was feeling something similar, without experiencing the guilty feeling of unfaithfulness to her dead husband that had usually accompanied such sensations in the past several months.

Both of them, though, were hesitant to say anything about those feelings just yet.

30

She sighed, watching her friend, Red Flower. She was still shivering under the furs piled on top of her. The solution didn't seem to be working.

She was afraid. Since she had been here at her friend's nest, she had been notified that Storm Cloud, the man she had treated a few nights before, had taken sick again and died. She racked her brain for anything that she could do, to improve the treatment she was administering.

"What would you do, mother?" she asked silently, imploring Golden Eye, the woman who had started her on this path years ago.

She had known from an early age that she was a quick learner, and that she was proficient at building on existing knowledge. She had greatly increased her expertise in healing during all the years that had passed since her mother had joined the Old Spirits.

Now, though, she felt helpless. She had never dealt with anything of this magnitude.

She did not remember her father, nor could she remember anything about the village they had lived in back then. It was somewhere north of here, only a few generations after her people had followed the game from the great land to the north and west. But she had heard the stories many times, of the great battle that took place. Many warriors had been killed, and the victors had taken the spoils, including women and children.

The man who had taken her mother after that had seemed a decent man, though it had taken her mother a long time to warm up to him. Nevertheless, in time, this village had become their home. Their medicine man had recently died, so some in the village considered themselves fortunate to have a medicine woman among them. Others were not happy with Golden Eye's new methods. But she diligently and conscientiously did the work for the village for the rest of her life. When she died all those seasons ago, that responsibility passed to her daughter.

She looked over at Red Flower's husband, Tall Tree, the eldest son of Stone Face, one of the village elders. Stone Face was one who had disapproved of Golden Eye. He believed that tribes should not mix, so Golden Eye had been a target of his displeasure for years. Golden Eye's new husband had served as a buffer between them, but after he was killed in a hunt, she had been forced to personally bear the brunt of Stone Face's anger on numerous occasions.

Stone Face felt that their reverence for the Old Spirits was what was necessary for their health and well-being. When Golden Eye introduced her foreign ideas about ingesting certain plants for medicinal purposes, it seemed to Stone Face like apostasy, a defection from their true beliefs. He thought that mixing physical 'medicine' with their long-held spiritual beliefs into some strange hybrid lifestyle demonstrated a lack of faith in the Spirits' ability to care for them. To Stone Face's dismay, the other elders were a little more tolerant.

As a child, she had only one friend, Honeybee, White Wolf's younger sister. Since Honeybee's father, Crow Feather, was another who was suspicious of Golden Eye's hybrid form of medicine, he was miserly with the time he allowed Honeybee to spend with her. Most of their play together was when he was away hunting. Therefore, she spent a great deal of time with her mother, learning the ways of the Old Spirits, and about the natural medicines that grew around them.

All the time she was growing up, she had witnessed Stone Face's enmity to an extent, but not to the degree that she began experiencing it herself after Golden Eye died. As she continued her mother's hybrid work, building on it, she often found herself at odds with the elder.

In fact, just a short time ago, he had come here to Tall Tree's and Red Flower's nest to object to her being there. Fortunately, she hadn't had to confront him herself. Tall Tree had gone out to face him, but she heard the argument. Stone Face accused his son of being disloyal to the Old Spirits by allowing these new false and treasonous practices into his home.

Having grown up with that attitude being expressed, it was nothing new, but it always hurt. She had spent almost all her life feeling like an outcast.

She looked over at Tall Tree now. He had finally fallen asleep. He had been so worried about Red Flower that he had scarcely slept the night before. He was exhausted. And the stress of his confrontation with his father probably didn't help.

She noticed he was shivering.

Tears filled her eyes as hopelessness engulfed her heart.

§

She heard footsteps approaching outside, followed by a tapping on the support stick for the nest. She glanced once more at Red Flower, then at Tall Tree. She had mixed some medicine for him and had him swallow it a few minutes ago. There was nothing more she could do now except wait. She turned and went out the opening in the shelter.

She smiled with relief when she saw White Wolf's face. Her relief was short lived.

"Birdsong," he said, his face lined with worry and sadness, "a lot of people have been looking for you. This ailment is overtaking our village."

"Have you not been able to help them?" she asked. White Wolf, as a boy, had been an assistant to the old medicine man. He had also helped Birdsong in her work on numerous occasions and was proving to be an able student.

"I'm afraid I don't yet have the knowledge or skills for what they need." He related to her a list of several villagers who were sick, and a few who had already died, including a couple of their friends.

"I must gather more medicine," she sighed, trying hard to hold back the tears so that she could focus on her objective. "I wonder if the Maker is angry with us."

"I don't know," he replied, "but there are some who are saying bad things about you."

"And I suppose Stone Face is the one whipping them up," she said bitterly.

"I don't know," he said, but Birdsong thought the look in his eyes said otherwise. "But you're supposed to be our link to the spirit world, and they are thinking that the Old Spirits have abandoned us."

"White Wolf, I'm doing everything I know how," she replied indignantly, wondering if his accusing tone was his own, or if he was simply expressing the others' thoughts. "The Spirits have not told me of anything new that I should be doing."

"That's what they're talking about. They think the Spirits have broken apart from you."

She looked at him for a few moments, and she felt the tears coming. His face expressed a mixture of emotions including, she thought, the anguish that he felt, not only for the friends lost, but also for Birdsong's pain.

"I don't believe it, though," he was quick to add. "I know of your devotion to the Old Spirits. I know you are doing everything that you can to save us from this sickness."

"I am," she nodded. "But it may not be enough. I don't know if I can turn it back."

"I know you can," he said, his voice taking on a more confident tone. "I know of your power. I am constantly in awe of your strength and knowledge."

The tears filled her eyes at that, and she leaned into White Wolf, drawing strength from his arms wrapped around her. She took a deep breath and pulled away.

"I must go," she said. White Wolf nodded and let go of her. "I will go to the Spirit Circle, to commune with the Old Spirits, and I must gather more medicine." She reached inside the shelter and picked up her leather pouch. She took a burning stick from the fire to quickly start a new one in the Spirit Circle. Then, with one last look at White Wolf, the afternoon sun shining copper in his hair and beard, she turned and went outside the village, beginning her climb up the mountain.

§

The Spirit Circle where Birdsong went to commune with the Old Spirits was a level clearing in the forest, up the mountain from the village and toward the west. The forest grew dense up the mountainside, and in this area, the trees were particularly thick. The clearing in the midst of it was a small space, barely a clearing at all, but it was a powerful place. The spiritual energy here was intensified by numerous talismans and charms arranged around the perimeter, links to the Old Spirits. The trees that ringed the clearing arched overhead, allowing only a scattered sprinkling of sunshine on the earth around her.

Those in the village knew that this was her place, and her mother's before her, for contacting the Spirits and, for the most part, they respected it. For years, now, any trails they made through the forest gave this little clearing a wide margin, by a distance of several paces, at her mother's request.

She sat cross-legged on the ground, amid the charms, with a small fire burning in front of her. She was hungry, but she didn't want to eat. Fasting sharpened one's senses, improving one's communion with the Spirits. She told herself to be patient. With her village dying around her, she hated to take too much time away, but it was important that she spend as much time as it took with the Spirits to get the answers she needed.

She looked across the fire, to the primary talisman that faced her, the skull now bleached clean and white. Her mother had presided here, watching over her for years during her consultations with the Spirits, but Birdsong had never faced as troubling a burden as she did now.

As her little fire died down to embers, she untied a leather thong on the front of her sleeveless upper garment and pulled her arms out of it, leaving it open but draped over her shoulders. She picked up a handful of Spirit's Breath, the dried plants she had laid out on the ground beside her, and placed them on the glowing coals. As a thick smoke drifted up, she pulled her garment up over her head and leaned into the smoke, catching it in her makeshift canopy. She inhaled and exhaled several times until the plants were reduced to ash.

She leaned back, dropping the garment behind her, and she picked up a sparkling clear crystal from among the talismans scattered about. Holding it with the tips of her fingers on both hands, she pressed it against her forehead, between her eyes, and rocked back and forth, her eyes closed to her surroundings, her mind open to direction from the Spirits.

"Old Spirits," Birdsong intoned, "please appear before me. Lead me in this trying time. I seek your wisdom and guidance."

She sat there, swaying back and forth for nearly an hour, her mind open to their direction.

But the Spirits were silent.

By now, the fire had died down, but the coals were still hot, so she dropped some more of the Spirit's Breath on them. She pulled the garment over her head again to catch the smoke, breathing it until the dried plants stopped smoking. Then she repeated her earlier actions, rocking back and forth with the quartz crystal pressed against her forehead.

"Please, mother," she entreated, "I need help. Please bring the Spirits to me. I can't do this alone."

Birdsong felt dizzy and light-headed, as the sun gradually passed overhead. Her stomach churned and growled, and while the hunger was unpleasant, she hoped it would make her more receptive to guidance from the Old Spirits.

But again, there was no response from the Spirits.

She sighed and put her hand out over the ashes of her fire. There was little heat coming off of it. She picked up some twigs and stirred up the ashes, finding a few little coals still glowing among them. She dropped dried grasses and twigs on them, blowing across it until a flame popped into life.

She stared into the little flames for several minutes, focusing her mind on her objective, opening her heart to the Spirits. As the flame turned once again to glowing embers, Birdsong dropped the remainder of the dried Spirit's Breath on the ash-covered coal. They lay there for a few moments before finally popping into flame, and she breathed deeply, inhaling as much of it as she could, her eyes burning.

As the sun dipped toward the hills to the west, Birdsong sat in the deep shadow the trees cast over her, the only light being the glow of the embers in front of her. Rocking unsteadily back and forth, the crystal was warm against her forehead, and she felt a measure of hope.

She heard a rustling sound from the forest ahead of her, and she put her head back, welcoming the Spirits. Keeping the crystal pressed against her forehead, she moved her hands up so that she could open her eyes and see them.

She saw several dark figures climbing up and pushing through the foliage, illuminated by the glowing embers of her fire. Everything looked blurry again, but at least this time, she understood why. She squinted at them, hoping to clear her vision.

The figures came closer and she took the crystal from her forehead, trying to bring them into focus.

"Birdsong," one of them said. His voice was familiar. "You must go."

"Go where?" she asked.

"Away from our people. You are not welcome among us anymore."

She struggled to understand the statement, but her head was so murky. As she pondered the mandate, one of the others spoke, not waiting for her to respond.

"Tall Tree and Red Flower are dead!" he snapped, stepping forward, shaking his spear at her, his voice much less controlled than the first speaker. "You were among the last people in their nest. You gave them your bad medicine and they both died!" The first one grabbed his arm and pulled him back, attempting to calm him.

"Our people are dying," the first one said. "Rather than helping them, you are hastening their departure from this world. Those you've given medicine to have all died, and still we get sick."

As her clouded mind worked to understand, it was finally getting through to her that these were not the Spirits that she sought, but the elders from her village.

"But I'm your medicine woman," Birdsong protested. "I'm trying to help our people." Her words sounded to her as if she was mumbling, but she couldn't seem to control it.

"You're not helping them. We have someone who will be taking your place."

Though she could still not see them clearly, she could see the one in front, Fire Maker, the calmer one who had been speaking, come closer to her, his feet nearly touching her mother's skull.

"Why are the Spirits not striking you dead for desecrating this Spirit Circle?" she wondered aloud.

He ignored her question, but dropped something on the ground in front of her.

"White Wolf gathered up your things for you." Birdsong reached forward and recognized some of her meager possessions in the bundle. "You must not come back. You must make a nest elsewhere. Keep your bad spirits away from us."

She could barely keep her eyes open as the figures disappeared into the foliage once more. As Birdsong drifted into unconsciousness, she had one coherent thought.

She truly was an outcast now.

31

"Oh my god," Fin said softly as Suzy filled him in on the episode, "she's being shunned." Suzy looked at him sympathetically as she recalled that he was enduring something similar. She turned to face him.

"Have you tried making contact with your family since they started shunning you?" she asked, changing the subject just a bit.

"Oh, sure," Fin replied. His tone was nonchalant, but Suzy could see the hurt. "They let me know that, until I bring my immoral, demonic lifestyle in line with their beliefs, they can't have anything to do with me."

Suzy placed her hand gently on his arm.

"How are you handling that?"

Fin looked at Suzy with only the hint of a grin.

"By spending time with my beautiful ghost-whispering sexual goddess of a girlfriend."

Suzy raised her eyebrows at him.

"Sexual goddess?"

"I worship thee on the altar of my bed, babe."

"Hmm," Suzy replied, squirming a little, "keep talking like that and I may have to exact atonement!"

"I only hope that I may please thee well enough."

"Birdsong," Suzy said abruptly, settling back in her original position.

"Huh?" Fin looked at her for a moment, his features drawn together in confusion.

"Her name is Birdsong."

"Oh," he replied, the grin breaking out across his face as he realized she was changing the subject. Then, he became serious again. "What a lovely name."

"Yeah," Suzy said pensively. During the quiet moment that passed, her stomach growled audibly.

"You're hungry, aren't you?" Fin asked. He pulled his phone from its holster and pressed a button on the side of it. "No wonder! It's almost three o'clock, and we never had lunch."

"What's nearby?" Suzy asked.

"Restaurant-wise?" Fin laughed. "Nothing. Everything's at least a half hour away."

"God, you really are a loner! Okay, what's good within a half-hour's drive?"

"There's a good Mexican restaurant a half hour from here."

"Perfect."

§

There were more people in the restaurant than Suzy expected for a late afternoon. As they waited for a table, they perused menus near the front door. Suzy glanced up at Fin, and what she saw held her gaze. To come out to dinner, he had put on a Harris Tweed blazer, complete with elbow patches. He now leaned comfortably against the wall, one hand in his pocket, one ankle crossed over the other. As he looked at his menu, Suzy felt that warm tingle in her gut again.

The spell was temporarily broken when the hostess led them to a table. Having studied the menu, they already knew what they wanted, so they placed their orders right away. They had their drinks in minutes.

"This is a local place," Fin explained. "I used to live in a little dump just south of Denver. That was when I was married to Kay. We both loved Mexican food, so we went to the first Los Dos Potrillos that was near there on South Holly Street. After we got divorced, I moved into Highlands Ranch, and I was happy to find that a new Los Dos Potrillos had just opened up there. Now that I live way out here in the boonies, this is the closest one."

"So, there are three of these places, huh?"

"Wow, you're really good with numbers," Fin joked.

Suzy scratched her forehead with her middle finger as she sipped her Margarita.

"Actually, there are four," he smiled, "but the fourth one's in Parker, and I don't plan on moving there any time soon. But even at a half hour away, this is definitely worth the drive. Best Mexican food in the Denver area."

As if to prove the point, the waitress arrived and placed their food in front of them. They each delved into their respective dinners.

"Mmm!" Suzy said.

"You just made a yummy sound," Fin said with a grin, and in an unfamiliar voice.

"Okay," Suzy said after she swallowed, "that doesn't sound like you, so I'm guessing that's another one of your movie quotes."

"You guessed correctly. That was Gene Wilder in *Young Frankenstein*."

"The least you could do, considering Birdsong's episodes, is quote from *Dances With Wolves*, or something like that."

"Oh come on, Suzy, that would be so out of place," Fin said. "Everyone knows that Kicking Bird and Wind In His Hair were Plains Indians." He smiled at her and Suzy shook her head and went back to eating her dinner, but then she looked thoughtfully at Fin.

"I *am* sorry about all the time I'm spending in these episodes," she said.

"Don't be sorry," Fin waved it off. "It's important stuff."

Suzy placed her hand on his. Fin was only too happy to hold her hand for a few moments, until she needed it back for eating.

"Besides," he continued, "it may ultimately help me, too, if I get a story out of it."

"That *would* be cool. Do you think Jennifer Lawrence will play me in the movie?"

"I can't think of anybody else who has a sufficient level of smartassedness to pull it off."

"And I suppose Ryan Reynolds would play you?"

"Of course. He's got the wit, the charm and the boyish good looks."

Suzy looked at him with a smile and with one eyebrow raised.

"Well, okay," Suzy said, "if it will help the cause, then I'll continue with Birdsong's story."

"Sounds good. But if you're really concerned about me, maybe you could do it naked. At least that would make it more interesting for *me*."

32

Clouds were swirling overhead, and Birdsong wondered where she was, considering the canopy of the forest was no longer above her. She lay on the ground, out in the open at the top of a hill, looking up for a few moments as the clouds darkened and churned over her.

Suddenly, immediately above her, the clouds blew apart, as if pushed out from behind, and a bright light shone through the center of the opening, warming her face and body. She lifted a hand to shield her eyes. Out of this light, a large eagle swooped down toward Birdsong, its immense wings casting a shadow across her, chilling her once again.

As the eagle came closer, Birdsong could see something in its talons. Its wings thrashing the air, blowing Birdsong's hair behind her, it slowed as it neared the ground. As it came closer, it opened its claws, dropping its burden just before touching down in front of her.

Her body warmed again by the light shining on her from above, Birdsong pushed herself upright, looking closely at the eagle. She gazed into the eagle's golden eye, after which her mother had been named.

"Have you come to help me, mother?" Birdsong asked, her heart filling with emotion.

"I have, child," the eagle replied. "These will help." The eagle bent her head down toward the things she had been carrying, then looked piercingly at Birdsong.

"How much?" Birdsong asked. "How do I mix it?"

"You will know," the eagle replied. "I will guide your heart. You must be strong and prevail."

At that, the eagle spread her wings, beating them against the air, and lifted herself up off the ground. She flew upwards in a great spiral, into the center of the light. As she disappeared into the white glare, the clouds closed behind her, leaving Birdsong once again in shadow.

Birdsong looked at the things the eagle had left behind on the ground. She recognized everything, the pinkish-purple flowers with the spiky centers, the dark purple, almost black, berries, the little white bulbs and a piece of honeycomb.

Finally, she felt as if there might be hope.

§

Birdsong pushed herself up from the ground. Once again, she was in the forest, in her Spirit Circle. The fire was dead. She looked around in momentary confusion, trying to regain her bearings. Looking up, she saw that the sky was dim through the trees of the clearing. Sunrise was near.

She didn't see the things that her mother had dropped for her in her vision. She did see the things that the village elders had left, though, and the memory came rushing back.

She was a woman without a home.

Maybe if she defeated this illness that was killing her people, she could win them over again.

There were a few thoughts troubling her mind. One was White Wolf. Fire Maker said that White Wolf had gathered up her things for them, but he didn't say what his attitude had been. Did he object to their decision concerning her? Did he stand up for her and resist them, or did he believe their allegations about her and submit willingly?

The other thing that troubled her was the elder's statement that they were arranging for someone to take her place as a healer. While Birdsong felt a measure of concern about her position among them, she was even more concerned about the welfare of her people, and she knew of nobody in the village who had the necessary skills.

She couldn't let herself think about that, though. She had to focus her attention on her objective. She had work to do. She brushed the tears from her eyes and pushed herself up off the ground.

Her bow and a small quiver of arrows was there. There was also additional clothing wrapped in a skin and tied with a leather strap, as well as a waterskin. She shivered in the early morning chill, so she picked up her upper garment from behind her and pulled it on, tying it closed with the leather thong in front. She picked up the bundle, slinging it over her shoulder. Her medicine pouch and the waterskin went over her other shoulder, and she picked up the bow and arrows. She needed to get busy searching for the supplies she needed.

33

"Echinacea," Suzy related, as Fin poured a second glass of Cabernet, "dark purple berries, I think elderberries, something that looked like garlic, and honey."

"Interesting," Fin replied, handing her a glass. "They all have either antibiotic or antibacterial properties."

"Really?" Suzy asked, looking at Fin in surprise. "How do you know that?"

"I do research," he shrugged. "I'm a writer. We know a little about a lot of stuff."

"Huh. Well, either the smoke she was breathing was particularly mind-expanding, or that vision quest thing really worked."

"I don't know," Fin replied as they made their way to the family room. "I like to think I have an open mind, but I admit I've never really looked into vision quests. Of course, in my past life, it would have been considered pursuit of the demons, but I think I've gotten beyond that now."

Sitting down on the loveseat, they clinked glasses, both apparently lost in their thoughts, and they each took a sip of their wine.

"However," Fin said, "I have my doubts about her cure. I don't know how those ingredients could defeat such a virulent contagion."

"But you just said that they all have antibiotic or antibacterial properties," Suzy countered, confused at his sudden doubts.

"That's true, but low-grade. By today's standards, they'd be very weak antibiotics. They'd be good for natural protection, daily maintenance, but they wouldn't do anything to kill an existing infection."

"Well," Suzy replied, contemplating, "maybe viruses a couple hundred of years ago were weaker. After all this time, and all the modern drugs we've pumped into ourselves, viruses have had a long time to build up immunities.

And maybe the human immune system was different back then, as well. Maybe it wouldn't have required as virulent of a contagion to kill them, or as strong a medicine to kill the disease."

"Huh," Fin said thoughtfully, "those are good points. I guess there could be a combination of factors working in Birdsong's favor."

"She's so distraught," Suzy said, her face drawn with worry. "She's bravely pressing on, but I could feel how heavy her heart was as she came out of the vision quest and remembered the elders banishing her."

"It's tough," Fin agreed. "Pretty much all of my friends were in my parents' church, and they all supported each other in the decision. I remember how panicked I felt when I realized that I had lost all my friends and family in one day. As I said, being an introvert likely helped me to adapt more quickly than some, but I don't know if that was the case with Birdsong."

"She doesn't feel like an introvert," Suzy said, scrunching her eyebrows together as she remembered what she felt in the episode.

"Yeah, so it may be harder for her."

Suzy thought for a moment.

"You know something I just realized?" she said. "There are no animals in this village. When did the Utes get horses?"

"I don't know exactly," Fin replied, looking into the distance as he pondered. "I think it was Cortes who brought them to the Americas sometime in the 1500s. I'm not sure how long it took them to breed and spread northward from Mexico. By the time they got up to the Utes, it may have been mid to late 1600s."

"Interesting. I think this is before they had horses."

"Wow. So Birdsong's been hanging around for quite a while." Fin looked at Suzy. "I wonder if her memory was murky."

"What do you mean?"

"Well," he paused, "mind you, this is purely speculation on my part."

"Honey, it's *all* speculation at this point," Suzy assured him. "It's not like the afterlife is any kind of hard science that people can do a hands-on study of. Come on, let's hear it."

"Okay, so Birdsong has been isolated on that mountain for maybe four hundred years, if our estimates are close, based on the horses. No interaction with anybody. If, as you said, she doesn't seem like an introvert, what could she do to keep from going crazy? I mean, can ghosts go into hibernation? Go dormant, so to speak?"

Suzy smiled as she heard the words, the almost naïve-sounding ideas he was applying to a ghost. But the more she thought about it, it did seem to make some kind of sense to her.

"So," she continued his thought, "when you brought the spearhead down off the mountain and brought it into your house, it stirred her for the first time in centuries. She woke up in this strange, modern structure, disoriented, maybe even groggy in some way."

"Exactly," Fin said, nodding his head. "That could account for why your initial episodes with her were blurry and muffled. After several hundred years, the memories were fuzzy to her, so the scenes were blurry to you. As she became more alert, your connection with her became more solid."

"So," Suzy replied, remembering an earlier point that Fin had made, "what I'm seeing is before the white man affected their lives."

"Lucky for them," Fin said.

"Lucky for you, too," Suzy replied. "You were worried she was an Indian with a grudge against whites."

"Huh. Just think, you and I are Birdsong's introduction to white people."

"Let's try to make a better impression than our ancestors did through the ages."

In an almost impulsive action, they leaned toward each other and gave each other a kiss, pulling each other close as they sipped their wine.

34

Within minutes, she had already found a patch of garlic and she dug up some of the bulbs and put them in her pouch. Having so quickly gotten a quarter of what she needed, she was feeling encouraged. She knew she could count on her mother to help her with a plan of action.

She knew the purple flowers grew in the sunshine at the edge of the forest. As she walked through the woods, her eyes were alert to any of the other things she needed, as well as to any dangers that she needed to avoid.

And food. She realized when she saw several rabbits ahead of her that she hadn't eaten anything in two days, and she was hungry. Her fast had been sufficient for making contact with the Old Spirits, but it wasn't necessary to continue it now.

She slowly selected an arrow and fitted it to the bowstring, pulling it back. She was not proficient with the bow, but White Wolf had been teaching her. She called to mind his instruction as she sighted along the arrow, selecting one of the rabbits as her target.

She took a breath, released it, and let go of the bowstring. As the arrow impaled her target, the other rabbits disappeared into the woods.

She could see White Wolf's approving smile in her memory, congratulating her on a good shot. The memory brought a tear to her eye, but she brushed it away and forced a smile.

In a few minutes' time, Birdsong had butchered the rabbit and started it roasting over a new fire that she had laboriously started herself. As it cooked, she examined the area around her makeshift camp for any of the other items she needed, but she found nothing useful.

As she ate her simple meal, she wondered how she would know how much of the ingredients to use. She remembered her mother's words to her in her vision. "You will know. I will guide your heart. You must be strong and prevail." She hoped that she would be alert to her mother's guidance when the time came.

§

Even though she had been quite hungry, she wasn't able to eat all of the large rabbit, so she wrapped the remainder in the skin and buried it just outside the Spirit Circle.

The sun was arching overhead when she reached the edge of the forest, where she remembered seeing the purple flowers in the past. She saw them just ahead of her, and she pulled several of them, roots and all. She bent the long stems several times and stuffed them in her pouch with the garlic.

Bees were all over the flowers, buzzing around in the sunshine, and she spent some time watching them, following ones that were particularly laden with pollen. She chafed at the time it was taking, knowing that, while she was doing this, others in her village were likely getting sick.

And dying.

But she tried not to think about that. She needed to stay focused on her goal. And giving her attention to the bees, and following them, would help her do that.

Eventually, she found their hive in a dead tree standing alone on the hillside and, after again building a small fire to produce some smoke, she managed to take a portion of the honeycomb.

She found a plant with large leaves and wrapped the honeycomb up in several of them. She was feeling particularly encouraged. She had the majority of the things she needed to make the medicine.

She knew that the berries were down in the valley to the south, growing near the river, so that's where she headed next. She made her way down the hillside, picking her way carefully through the brush, but still, her legs were getting scratched up from the thorny brush that grew on the hill.

She was glad when she finally reached the river. Rushing eastward from the mountains, the icy river formed a formidable barrier to the country south of there, and she was relieved that the berries she sought grew on both sides of the river.

Birdsong approached one of the bushes laden with the dark purple berries, and she crouched down to pick as many as she could. As the river roared past over the rocks, she focused on her task. She didn't hear the rustling of the brush nearby. When she had picked all the berries from that bush, she stood up and turned, startling the huge brownish-grey beast to her right, drinking from the river. The breeze had been blowing across the river, and neither had caught the scent of the other.

The animal lifted its trunk out of the river and trumpeted loudly, its enormous curved tusks soaring high in the air above Birdsong. Flapping its ears in alarm, the creature shook its giant head back and forth.

Birdsong stepped back slowly, clutching her leather pouch to her breast, even more precious now that it contained all of the ingredients to the cure for the illness afflicting her people. Backed up now against the bushes surrounding her, she stood her ground, careful to make no moves that might be perceived as threatening.

After a terrifying show of alarm, the beast gave one last warning trumpet, then turned and quickly plodded away.

Birdsong exhaled the breath that she had been holding, and her knees gave way as she plopped down onto the ground in a faint.

35

Fin knew something was going on before Suzy came out of the episode. She had gotten ready for bed, but decided to go under one more time before going to sleep. But based on what she was apparently witnessing in this one, judging by her tensed muscles and her gasping for breath, Fin figured she was going to have a hard time getting to sleep.

He had been sitting against his headboard, kneading the pain that had lingered in his head ever since they went out to dinner, when he noticed Suzy's distress. He turned to face her, noting the creases in her forehead from her eyebrows pushed up as high as they would go. He saw her lips quivering, slightly parted, her cheeks twitching. Fin had never seen an episode affect her this strongly, and he felt alarmed.

He took her hand, waiting for the recognition to return to her eyes. When it finally did, Suzy jumped, pressing herself back against the headboard, her eyes wide with panic. Fin was afraid she was going to hyperventilate.

"Baby," he said in a calm voice, "it's okay. You're safe. It's all over."

It took a few seconds, but when she recognized Fin, she threw her arms around him, holding him tightly. He held her and rocked her, stroking her back until her breathing slowed.

After a minute or so, Fin felt her arms loosen their grip, and he let her sit back against the headboard.

"Sweetie, what was it? What did you see?"

"It was a ma—a mammoth, or a mastodon. Something like that."

"You - wait, what? A mammoth?"

"It was huge! And it was just a few feet away."

"Okay," Fin said carefully, "honey, it's not that I don't believe you, but - well, describe to me exactly what you saw."

Suzy concentrated on taking a deep, slow breath, and then exhaling it completely. She looked at Fin.

"It was brownish-grey with thin fur, and it was – god, it was probably about twenty feet tall! It had a long, muscular trunk and these enormous, curved tusks that had to be at least twelve feet long. And the sound it made!" She put her hands against her ears at the memory. "It was terrifying!"

Fin was having a little trouble processing what Suzy had said. His first attempt at calm logic failed.

"Okay, I'm sure it was terrifying," he said, "but as close as you were, it probably just *seemed* bigger and scarier."

"What?" Suzy looked at him in disbelief.

"Don't get me wrong," Fin said, raising his hands in a calming gesture, "I understand that what you saw was big. But you were at close range and frightened, and your mind probably amplified what you saw. Couldn't you have seen a modern-day elephant?"

"Fin," Suzy said, peering intently into his eyes, "do you really think an elephant roaming the valley around Silver Plume, Colorado is more logical?"

"I – no, it's not," he replied with a sigh, seeing the fallacy of his jumped-to conclusion.

"I know what I saw!" Suzy insisted. "This thing was hairy, and when it finally walked away, its back wasn't rounded like an elephant, but it sloped downward from the shoulders. It *resembled* an elephant, but there were definite differences, too."

"You're right," he said, shaking his head. "It's just that – well, this . . . this is crazy. I mean we were talking about these episodes being maybe four hundred years ago. Mammoths haven't been around here in *thousands* of years!"

Fin got out of bed and began pacing nervously around it.

"This is not . . . it's not – how can –" He closed his eyes and rubbed his head for a moment. "You –" He finally stopped and sighed in frustration and looked at Suzy, concentrating on constructing a complete sentence. "You're telling me that this ghost is *thousands* of years old?" he asked, pointing in the direction of his hobby room. "Is that even possible?"

"I'm just telling you what I saw, Fin," Suzy replied, trying hard to remain calm. "I don't know anything about mammoths or the time period they lived in or how long a ghost can stick around, but I know what I saw."

Fin looked at her for several seconds, as she yawned, likely from a combination of stress and exhaustion.

"Right," he finally said. "Okay, let's . . . let's try to get some sleep and we'll see if we can figure this out in the morning."

§

After a night with not much sleep for either one of them, they made the forty-five minute drive to the University of Denver in south Denver. They walked into Marty Keating's classroom, as arranged on the phone call that Fin had made earlier, forty-five minutes before his class was scheduled to start.

"O Captain! My Captain!" Fin called as they entered the classroom. Keating looked up and pushed his dark hair back, rolling his eyes as if the greeting was an old and overused joke.

"Hi, Fin," he said, putting out his hand. "It's good to see you again."

"You too, Marty," Fin said, shaking his hand. "And this is Suzy Quinn."

"Pleased to meet you," she said as they shook hands.

"Very nice to meet you too, Suzy," Keating smiled.

"Captain?" she asked, looking from Fin to Keating and back.

"Professor Keating," Fin said in a tone that made it sound as if it was so obvious. "From *Dead Poet's Society*. Professor John Keating? Robin Williams?"

"Okay," Suzy said, "I've seen it. I didn't remember that was his name."

"Fin thinks it's really clever," Keating said with a sigh, "to greet me that way ever since re-watching that movie after I got my Doctorate."

"I knew Marty from college," Fin explained, "but we haven't really kept in close touch with each other since then, just getting together now and then."

"Well, we're kind of in two different worlds," Keating said. "Fin went on to compose stories in his fictional realms, while I stayed firmly rooted in the facts of the past."

"He's a history major, like you," Fin explained to Suzy.

"Yeah, I usually only hear from Fin when he wants information about an arrowhead he's found."

"Marty teaches classes on Native American history." Fin turned to Keating. "We really should get together more often." As he was saying it, his inner introvert was admitting to himself that it was not likely.

"Well," Keating said with a glance at the clock, "let's see this arrowhead."

"Actually, I think it's a spearhead," Fin said, as Suzy gingerly pulled it out of her purse, wondering where Birdsong was at that moment. She held it out to Keating. His eyes widened a little as he took it carefully in his hands.

"Oh, my!" he said quietly. He took it to his podium and switched on the light, turning the spearhead over and over, examining it carefully. "This is remarkable!"

"Yeah, it's a beautiful piece," Fin agreed.

"Where did you find it?"

"On a trail a little ways above Silver Plume." Fin glanced at Suzy, then back at Keating. "Is it Ute?"

Keating looked up at Fin.

"No," he said, and he looked back down at the spearhead. "No, this is not within my realm of expertise." He looked at it a few seconds longer, then looked up at Fin and Suzy. "You need to speak with Professor Windsor." He glanced at the clock again. "He should be here now. Come with me."

He started out the door of his classroom, and Fin and Suzy followed.

"Who's Professor Windsor?" Fin asked as they hurried behind him. "Professor of what?"

"Professor of Anthropology. He has a particular interest in paleontology."

Fin saw what looked like a smug expression on Suzy's face.

§

Professor Windsor studied the spearhead through the reading glasses perched precariously close to the end of his nose. He was over six feet tall, but stood a bit shorter with the slouch that had been with him for the last few decades. His hair was grey and receding, but it fell forward onto his high forehead as he hunched over the spearhead.

"Extraordinary," he said in a hushed tone.

"Yes, I thought you would find this interesting," Keating said.

"What can you tell us about it, Professor?" Fin asked after allowing Windsor several moments to examine it.

"Well, from a number of characteristics, the size of it, the lanceolate shape, the fluting on the base –"

"Wait, sorry," Suzy said, "what does that mean? Lanceolate shape?"

"Yes, that refers to the lance head shape. It's rather long, and wider in the middle than on the point or the base."

"Okay," Fin said, "and the fluting you mentioned? What do you mean by that?"

"You see how it's hollowed out a little here at the base," he explained patiently but enthusiastically. He pointed to an indentation beginning about halfway down the length of the stone, and continuing the remaining three inches to the base. "You see these on both sides," and he turned it over, showing an identical feature on the other side. "This is where a split wooden shaft would be hafted onto the stone, making quite a formidable weapon."

Windsor was already distracted again, though, closely studying the spearhead, muttering "extraordinary." But Fin was impatient.

"Can you do carbon dating on it or something, to see how old it is?" he asked.

"Oh, no," Windsor said, looking up at Fin, "radiocarbon dating would not tell us anything about this."

"Why not?" Fin asked.

"I'm afraid radiocarbon dating is only for use on once-living matter. Dead animals, bones, plants, things like that. You see, carbon-14 is a radioactive isotope that's absorbed by living things throughout life, by ingestion, respiration, and so on. As long as the organism is alive, it contains the same proportion of carbon-14 as the atmosphere around it.

"After death, though, the organism will cease absorbing carbon-14. The amount of it remaining in the tissues can be measured, and since we know how long it takes for carbon-14 to decay, an approximate date of the death of the organism can be determined. But a piece of stone was never alive, so carbon dating it would tell us nothing."

Windsor was already closely scrutinizing the spearhead again. Keating, though, noticed the crestfallen look on Fin's face.

"There are other ways to tell, though," he said. "I believe Professor Windsor was about to speak of that."

"Yes," Windsor said, his attention again diverted from the spearhead, "you're right. I was." He cleared his throat and looked back down at it. "Various physical characteristics – the shape of it, the workmanship and style, all point to it being a very fine example of a Clovis point."

"Clovis point?" Suzy asked.

"Yes, it's named after the place where the first ones were found, near Clovis, New Mexico, back in 1929, I think. But specimens of Clovis points have been found in numerous places across the United States since then."

"But can you determine how old it is?" Fin asked.

"Not with any absolute degree of certainty, without being able to examine where it was found, the depth of the strata it was in, other artifacts in the vicinity."

"The depth?" Fin said. "It was on the surface, only partially buried in the dirt on the hillside."

"Ah," Windsor said, "well, then it's likely that erosion on the hillside over time may have washed away layers of soil from above the spearhead, eventually bringing it up to the surface."

"Okay," Fin said, feeling discouraged, "so there's no way to know how old this is?"

"It can't be pinpointed, as I said, with absolute certainty. But Clovis points are known to have been made in the late Pleistocene era, roughly twelve to thirteen thousand years ago.

§

"Columbian mammoth," Suzy said as they neared Fin's home. On their way back, she had been using her phone to do research on what she could find about mammoths. Several of the recreations she saw were similar to what she had witnessed in the episode, but the Columbian mammoth matched most closely.

As Fin pulled into his garage, she showed him the illustration in Wikipedia. Fin raised his eyebrows and whistled softly.

"They inhabited the Americas," Suzy said, "from the northern United States down to Costa Rica during the Pleistocene era. They were one of the largest species of mammoth, standing thirteen feet at the shoulder and weighing 22,000 pounds!"

"Damn!" Fin said. He looked at Suzy. "Can I just say that I appreciate you not being an asshole?"

"Oh, well yes, that's one of my finest qualities," Suzy replied quite seriously. Then, she smiled as she pinched her eyebrows together in bewilderment. "What the hell are you talking about, Fin?"

"You could have held an 'I told you so' attitude over my head the whole way back, but you haven't."

"Well, I might have reconsidered if you hadn't so quickly admitted you were wrong."

"It's difficult to hold on to a belief or attitude in the face of opposing facts."

Suzy scoffed at this.

"There are a surprising number of people in the world who still manage to do it." Suzy's expression warmed. "I appreciate the fact that you're not one of them."

Fin leaned over and kissed her. He started to get out of the car, then he stopped.

"Where do you suppose Birdsong is?" he asked.

"You know, I wondered the same thing when we were at DU."

"I mean, does she fit in your purse with the spearhead? Did she ride in the back seat?"

"Maybe she was on your lap," Suzy suggested. She smiled at the flash of panic on his face.

36

"Well," Suzy said when she joined Fin in his hobby room, "after multiple unsuccessful attempts to reestablish contact with Birdsong, I think it's safe to say that she's pissed." Fin had just placed the spearhead back in the prominent, central position of his collection.

"I'm sorry," he replied. "Do you think she's gone?"

"Where would she have gone?"

"I don't know. To the next place?"

"After twelve thousand years, I think it's safe to say that she probably isn't going to move on without some coaxing or instruction."

"Maybe we left her at DU."

Suzy thought for a moment about that idea. There were numerous artifacts in both professors' work areas. Professor Windsor, especially, had quite an extensive collection, many of his specimens going back to an era contemporary with Birdsong's.

"I don't know," she finally said. "I don't think a spirit would just transfer to another place or artifact on a whim. I think I'm just back at square one with her." She looked at Fin with a sad expression on her face. "Can you imagine how traumatic it would be to be taken from the Pleistocene Era into the 21st century, only to be jerked into yet another foreign location without any consideration of your feelings? I can't imagine what she must be feeling now."

"Yeah, I never thought about that," Fin said sympathetically, as he carefully closed the glass cover over his arrowhead collection. "Well, I'm sure you'll get her back. You made a connection with her. I think that must involve some level of trust."

"I guess so. I just feel really bad for her. She's been through so much already."

"I know." Fin put his arm around Suzy's shoulders as he walked her toward the door. "Just keep trying."

"Well, I feel guilty about that, too," Suzy said. "I came out here to spend time with you. Instead, I've ended up spending a good portion of my visit communing with two different ghosts, leaving you pretty much on your own."

"Don't worry, sweetheart, I've got stuff to do anyway. Starting with lunch. I'll make us some sandwiches. Keep trying, and I'll call you when they're ready."

"You're the best!" Suzy replied as she kissed him.

"No, *you* are." Fin smiled, and he left her there to go downstairs.

§

After making a couple more attempts to reestablish contact with Birdsong, and failing, Suzy decided to let it rest a while. She and Fin ate their lunch on his back deck, with a view of the foothills to the west.

After that, they went for a long walk along the trail behind his house, enjoying the warming sunshine of spring at the base of the Rocky Mountains. They were able to chat, exploring their relationship without distraction from others, living or dead.

They arrived back at his house holding hands. After Fin opened the door, he stopped Suzy, pressing her back against the door jamb, looking long and deep into her eyes. The kiss that followed brought a moan up from Suzy's throat.

"Oh my god," she said in a breathy voice, clutching his butt and pulling him close, "I wish I wasn't so damn sweaty now."

"Well, you know," he replied, as he nuzzled the side of her neck, "Colorado isn't quite the backwards Old West setting that a lot of people seem to think it is."

"Really?" Suzy asked, her body squirming in his arms.

"Yeah." He nibbled her earlobe. "We actually have running water and real showers."

"I'm intrigued," she managed to say, wrapping her leg around his. "Tell me about these showers."

"Well," he continued quietly, breathing softly into her ear, "you take off all your clothes and stand in there while warm water sprays all over your naked body."

"Mmm," Suzy replied.

Fin slipped his hand under her shirt at the small of her back, while his lips continued exploring down her jawline, toward the front of her neck.

"And is this a solitary activity," Suzy asked haltingly, barely able to speak above a whisper, "or one that is shared with others?"

"It's usually solitary," Fin said as he reached the front of her throat, "but in certain situations," he started moving downward, unbuttoning her blouse, "it can be shared with another individual." His face directly in front of her breasts, he planted a kiss in her cleavage.

Suzy put her hands on both sides of his face and pulled it up even with hers. She looked at him for several moments, her breathing ragged, her expression intense. Finally, she pulled him toward her and kissed him.

"Your lips are salty," she whispered when they parted.

"Your skin is salty."

"Will you wash it for me?"

"It would be my pleasure."

§

Suzy's hair still hung in damp ringlets around her face as she and Fin lay inches apart in his bed. They had little to say, but just spent the time staring into each other's eyes in the dimming light, caressing each other under the sheet. Having spent themselves on their long hike, their extended foreplay in the shower, followed by their lovemaking in bed, they were content now just being in each other's company.

In time, Fin was the one to break the silence.

"Your eyes look like a place I want to jump in and swim and just stay forever."

Suzy sighed.

"That image," she replied thoughtfully, her eyes feeling heavy, "is equal parts disturbingly creepy and heart-achingly romantic."

"Romantic is what I was going for," Fin said sleepily.

"I know," Suzy smiled, and she kissed him again. Fin couldn't resist her smile, and he sighed in return.

"I can't believe how lucky I am."

"I can't believe how tired I am."

Fin thought for a few moments, waiting for her remark to sink in to his sleepy brain.

"We kind of skipped dinner," he said. "Are you hungry?" Suzy pondered for a moment.

"I am, but I think I'm more sleepy than hungry."

"Yeah, me too," Fin mumbled. He reached behind him and turned his lamp off. He yawned, and Suzy responded by yawning herself. The shadows of their loved one's face was the last thing each of them saw as they drifted off to sleep.

§

Fin jerked his eyes open as he heard his door bang into the wall. His head pounded with the noise. He felt Suzy's hand on his shoulder, and knew she was awake, too.

The first thing he noticed was how cold his bedroom was. Despite the fact that he knew his furnace was running, his room felt frosty.

He looked toward the door and saw a translucent figure, a young woman, naked except for some kind of animal skin wrapped around her hips. She seemed fairly short, but had an athletic build, her body toned from her active lifestyle. Her face was attractive, her features resembling Inuit natives, her long dark hair pulled back and tied out of the way with a strip of leather.

While it was dark in the room, the clerestory window set in the eave of Fin's cathedral ceiling allowed the meager light of the stars to shine on the wall behind her. Fin noticed that she was not casting a shadow. The young woman seemed to be illuminated from within, or glowing on her surface, with a kind of aura shimmering around her, which gave the effect of waves of heat surrounding the glowing embers of a dying fire.

The expression on her face as she looked around the unfamiliar space was a little difficult to decipher. It could have been fear or anger. Possibly both.

Her expression wouldn't have bothered Fin quite as much if she hadn't been holding a bow with an arrow fitted to the string and ready to shoot. He had been holding his breath, and he started gasping for air, his head throbbing, when she turned toward him. Her shimmering aura turned fiery when she saw him. Fin's breathing intensified as he remembered the ghosts he had seen in the Edinburgh vaults, and in Suzy's carriage house the year before, and the ghostly inferno they precipitated when angry.

As Birdsong turned and lifted her bow toward Fin, her expression now became a little more discernible. The anger seemed to become the predominant emotion over the fear as she pulled the string back, aiming the arrow directly at Fin's chest.

"Wait! Stop!" Fin cried, putting his hand out, hoping to stop the arrow from impaling him. Then, he heard a string of gibberish from Suzy behind him. Surprised that he could take his eyes off the terrifying apparition in front of him, he turned to glance at Suzy. She was gazing intently at Birdsong, speaking to her, apparently, in her own language.

He turned to look back at Birdsong, who seemed to be listening to Suzy, and apparently just as surprised as Fin was to hear Suzy speaking in her language. She relaxed the bowstring a bit as she listened.

"What the hell's going on, Suzy?" Fin whispered breathlessly.

"She's upset," Suzy replied, her voice low and even, "as we suspected." Birdsong watched them both as they spoke, her face expressing her confusion at the strange words. "She was taken from the place she was familiar with and brought here. Just as she was starting to grow *somewhat* accustomed to here, we took her somewhere else. She's angry and she's afraid."

"I thought you said ghosts can't hurt us," Fin said, looking at the sharp stone arrowhead, trying to keep from going into a full-blown panic.

"According to what Leanne and Lilith told me, they can't. Not directly, anyway. So I don't know if a ghost's arrow would even do anything to you."

"Well, let's not find out, okay?" he replied, his eyes a little wild. "Remember my hypothermia after I was engulfed inside that ghost in the vaults? Apparently they can have *some* amount of physical effect on us."

Birdsong, her patience apparently growing thin at being kept waiting, pointed the arrow at Fin again, pulling the string taut.

As Fin scrunched up his face, dreading the impalement he feared was coming, Suzy spoke once more, putting her arm around Fin, and Birdsong relaxed her pull on the bowstring a bit. Her expression changed a little, as well. Fin thought she looked almost contrite, or apologetic.

Birdsong responded to Suzy, nodding her head, and she relaxed the bowstring completely. Suzy jabbered back at Birdsong. After a brief exchange, the prehistoric woman looked once more at Fin. Then, with a look of disdain, she turned and walked out of the room. Her legs moved as if taking steps, though her body moved smoothly as if she simply glided across the floor.

Fin collapsed back onto his pillow, his chest heaving as he panted for breath. Suzy blew out a heavy sigh of relief, and Fin looked at her in the darkness, as the room gradually warmed up again.

"What the hell was that?" he asked.

"Well," Suzy replied slowly as she caught her breath, "she was upset, as I said. I apologized to her and assured her that we didn't mean to disturb her. It was entirely by accident that we brought her here to your house, and that our trip to DU this morning was simply an effort to gather information.

"I promised her that we wouldn't move her again, unless it was to put her back in her forest, or help her to move on. She didn't seem to understand that last part. I'm not sure I was able to make myself very clear about that. I don't know how deep of a grasp I have of the vocabulary."

"Well, that's mainly what I was talking about," Fin said, pushing himself up to sit back against the headboard. He turned his bedside lamp on and took a deep breath, blowing it out as his breathing steadied. "I got the gist of what was being talked about. I'm just wondering how you *could* talk with her."

"It was your idea that making the psychic connection with her would allow me to understand what was being said in the episodes."

"Well, yeah, but being psychically linked so you understand thoughts that are expressed and being able to actually converse with someone in a foreign language are two very different things."

"I don't know," Suzy replied. She thought for a moment. "I remember something similar last year, when I made contact with Fiona at my place, and with Jimmy Campbell in Edinburgh. I understood words and expressions that I'd never heard before. And I even embarrassed myself a couple of times by speaking with a Scottish accent and vocabulary in front of others.

"I don't remember any of the words or expressions now, though," she added thoughtfully, "so maybe it's just a temporary effect of the connection."

"Well," Fin said, putting his head back against the headboard and closing his eyes, "I, for one, am glad that this was a possible side-effect."

"Are you okay?" Suzy asked.

"It looks like I am, thanks to you." His head was still throbbing, but he decided to not say anything about that. Having regained his breath and composure, he looked askance at Suzy. "So much for my effort to be less wimpy about your ghosts."

"Considering that you almost got a spectral arrow through your heart, I think this reaction can be forgiven."

"You didn't tell me she was so hot. And almost naked."

"I didn't know myself," Suzy responded, for the moment ignoring his teasing tone. "That was the first time I'd seen her. I haven't had a face-to-face with her. Only the episodes, which I see through her eyes." Then, she looked at him, adopting a sarcastic tone. "If you're interested, though, I'll see if I can set you up with the dead girl."

"That's okay," Fin smiled. "I think my chances are a little better with you."

"You're probably right," Suzy said nonchalantly. "At least I haven't tried to kill you." She looked back at him. "Yet."

37

Following her face-to-face confrontation with the mammoth, Birdsong shakily picked herself up off the ground. She looked around her, happy to see that her toils of the day had not been spoiled. Her leather pouch, now stuffed with the components of the medicine that she had gathered, had protected them when she fainted.

As long as she was here, she took her waterskin off her shoulder and refilled it from the river. Then, she picked up her medicine pouch. Looking all around her, not wanting to repeat the incident with the mammoth, she began climbing up the hill, back to her Spirit Circle on the mountain above the village, in the relative safety of the forest.

She spent the rest of the afternoon, and into the evening, mixing the ingredients, asking the Old Spirits for their guidance. She remembered the words of the eagle in her vision, spoken in her mother's voice, "You will know. I will guide your heart."

She made use of the knowledge that she already had about each of the ingredients. When she wasn't certain about an amount or a proportion, she closed her eyes and opened her heart, allowing herself to be guided by the Spirits.

At least, she hoped it was the Spirits, and not simply her imagination.

§

It was a warm evening. As the moonlight lit her path between the trees, Birdsong carefully made her way down the mountain toward the village. Her waterskin, now filled to bulging with medicine, hung heavy over her shoulder.

Birdsong knew she would be coming down on the north side of the village, and her nest was on the north side. She wondered who would be on guard duty at the north edge when she arrived. As she stealthily approached the edge of the village, she squinted to try to improve her vision, and she couldn't believe her good luck. It was White Wolf.

He heard Birdsong approach, and he raised his bow toward the sound, his eyes squinting as he scanned carefully into the night, stepping behind the trunk of a tree. When he saw Birdsong, he caught his breath and relaxed his bow.

"Birdsong," he said quietly, "you should not be here."

"White Wolf," she replied, her heart aching to hold him, "I have communed with the Old Spirits. I have a treatment for the illness that plagues our people." It had been days since she had been exiled from her village, but she felt so alone, it was as if she had been on her own for weeks!

White Wolf looked around, then nodded toward the cover of forest, allowing her to approach, replacing his arrow in his quiver as he followed her into the darkness.

"My mother visited me at the Spirit Circle," she said, as White Wolf put his arm around her, holding her tightly, "and she helped me to make strong medicine for our people." White Wolf shivered as he held Birdsong close to him. Birdsong felt that she had her answer about White Wolf's reaction to the elders and their exiling of her.

He looked down at the bulging waterskin hanging on its strap from Birdsong's shoulder. He pondered for a moment, then looked back at her, his face twisted with worry.

"The village elders held a council," he said. "They've consulted with several people in the village." White Wolf paused, his eyes expressing concern. When he spoke again, his voice was quiet. "They've banished you from our people."

"I know. They visited me at the Spirit Circle to tell me. And to bring me the things you gathered for me."

He looked a little embarrassed. Or ashamed.

"Stone Face insisted that you were engaged in dangerous communication with evil spirits. I told him, and the other elders, that you weren't, but they were insistent on banishing you. So I at least made sure you had everything you might need until you came back. I knew you would be successful."

"I was," Birdsong replied happily, earnestly, taking the waterskin off her shoulder and passing it to him.

"I must present it to the elders," he said.

"I know," she nodded. "I will return tomorrow, before noon. Meet me at our rock?" White Wolf nodded.

A thought occurred to Birdsong, and she squinted, struggling to see his face in the darkness.

"After this is over," she said, "why don't we go somewhere else?"

"Where?" he asked.

"I don't know," Birdsong replied. "But too many in this village are not open to new ideas. They only want to hold on to the old ways." She felt White Wolf bristle a little. "The old ways are fine," she added quickly, "but I believe the Maker wants us to better ourselves, to improve on the old ways."

"Maybe," White Wolf replied, a little doubtfully.

"What's wrong?"

White Wolf hesitated a few moments before replying.

"I suppose it must be easier for you," he finally said. "But my family is here. I would have to leave my father and my mother, my sister."

"I know," she responded. It often hurt to be reminded that she had virtually nobody here, but now was not the time to persist. She had greater things to worry about. "Alright, I'll meet you at our rock tomorrow."

He kissed her, leaning forward to see into her eyes in the dim light.

"My heart beats with yours," he said, pressing his forehead against hers.

"My heart is yours," she replied. After gazing into each other's eyes for several moments, they parted, and Birdsong climbed the mountain, back to her Spirit Circle.

Once she reached the clearing, she sat down beside her fire and stoked the embers, putting another log on top of it. She sat there catching her breath, remembering White Wolf's face, his words, his touch. As she stared into the flames, she could feel the tears filling her eyes and, having completed the work she had come to do, she finally allowed them to flow.

§

There was little heat coming off her fire when she woke in the morning. She stirred the embers, clearing off the ash, and she put another small log on it, blowing on it to coax the flame. She gazed blankly into it as she gradually woke up, pushing her fingers through her hair to pull out the pine needles and leaves that had collected there overnight.

She saw a large chipmunk on the ground several yards away, foraging between the trees, and her stomach growled in response. She hadn't eaten anything since the rabbit yesterday. Moving slowly, she picked up her bow and an arrow, aiming carefully. It was a little smaller than the rabbit she shot yesterday, which would make it the smallest target she had attempted, and she didn't want to waste her shot. It was big enough to fill her belly.

Breathing slowly, she sighted down the length of the arrow, held her breath, and let go of the string. Her arrow impaled the chipmunk, killing it instantly. She smiled, and she silently thanked White Wolf for his training.

A few minutes later, the body of her prey was cooking over her fire. She still had a few berries and some honey left, so she enjoyed a delicious breakfast after the meat had browned a bit.

As she ate, she remembered her brief time with White Wolf the night before, remembered the feel of his arms around her, and she looked forward to seeing him again soon. Her exile had only been in effect a few days, but now that she had made medicine for the sickness that was ravaging her village, she knew that it was soon to be over.

§

White Wolf was waiting for Birdsong beside their rock when she came down the next day. She ran to him and they slipped into the forest behind the tall boulder. Holding each other tightly, they each breathed deeply of the other's scent.

White Wolf cupped a hand over her buttock and pulled her up close to him as he kissed her, pressing her back against the rock. Birdsong held on to him tightly, relaxing her hold only enough to allow him to reach both hands down and push the skin down over her hips, letting it drop to her ankles.

She pushed away from the rock, turning to the side, and she slipped down to the ground, opening her upper garment. White Wolf looked down at her for a few moments, and Birdsong was aroused by his eyes as they moved over her body.

He dropped to his knees beside her, and he leaned over her, kissing her deeply, his hand caressing her body, from her breast down to soft folds between her legs. When she couldn't take it any longer, she pushed down the skin he wore and pulled him on top of her.

As he entered her, Birdsong, through the tears in her own eyes, saw tears in White Wolf's eyes, as well.

§

"I've missed you so much!" Birdsong said as they lay panting afterwards in each other's arms. Then she saw the tense expression on White Wolf's face. "What's wrong?"

"The elders have not ruled in your favor," he replied. "I insisted that you want to help us, but they wouldn't listen. When I told them that Golden Eye helped you make the medicine, it didn't sway them. They say that you threatened them up on the mountain."

"What?" Birdsong couldn't believe what she heard. "How did I threaten them?"

"Stone Face said that, when they arrived, you were performing the foreign magic that your mother brought from your old tribe, and that you told them to leave at once. When they didn't, you looked at each one of them, and your face changed into theirs, one by one, but angry. You spoke to each of them, in their voice, insisting that they leave you alone."

"Stone Face is lying, White Wolf," Birdsong insisted. "I did no such thing."

"His son died, and Red Flower."

"I know," Birdsong replied softly, "I remember."

"They said that, after that, you turned into a giant eagle and threatened to strike them dead if they did not leave your Spirit Circle."

"I can barely remember saying a single word to them," she said, vaguely remembering their visit. "I was seeking the Old Spirits' help at the time. But I'm quite certain I never turned into a giant eagle!"

White Wolf nodded, but Birdsong thought she might have seen a flash of doubt in his eyes.

"You seem upset," she said. He hesitated for a moment, but then, the tenseness returned.

"My mother is sick." Birdsong gasped at the news.

"White Wolf," Birdsong implored, getting up on her elbow, "give Moonlight some of the medicine! My mother appeared to me in my vision as an eagle and she helped me make it. You must help her!"

"An eagle?" White Wolf echoed, looking askance at her. "Like Stone Face said?"

"My mother, Golden Eye. White Wolf, she was named after the far-seeing eye of the eagle. You know this. The elders know this." She looked at him anxiously. "White Wolf, you know me. Do you doubt me?"

He looked at her for several seconds, his chest rising and falling as he struggled with his thoughts.

"They said that you are using the magic of bad spirits that your mother brought from your old village to the north. The elders are here to protect us. They are appointed by the Old Spirits. Why would they lie about this?"

"I don't know, White Wolf. But I promise you that I didn't do those things they're saying I did."

His face blurred as tears filled her eyes.

38

"I wonder if Stone Face's lies about Birdsong eventually became the basis of the skin-walker legend," Fin said over breakfast, after Suzy had related the episode to him.

"Skin-walker?" Suzy echoed. "I've heard the term, but I don't know what it is."

"I don't know much about it, either, other than what was related in horror movies about it. And knowing horror movies, I don't suppose they concerned themselves too much with maintaining accuracy in relating the original Native American legends. I imagine they were bent around quite a bit to fit the stories the film-makers wanted to tell.

"But I think it's something like a shape-shifter, a witch who could take on the form of other creatures. I'm sure there was usually killing involved, but again, I don't know details. Seems like there were similar stories among several Native American tribes."

"Interesting," Suzy said a little distantly.

"You're a history major. I figured you'd know about this stuff."

"My knowledge of history centered mainly on European history and their eventual migration to America." Suzy looked pensive for a moment. "What originally got me fired up about history was a class on the Visigoths and the sacking of Rome."

"Hmm. I'll bet the class didn't cover the Invisigoths," Fin quipped as he put a forkful of eggs in his mouth.

"The Invisigoths?" Suzy asked, raising her eyebrows at him.

"Sure. You can't see them, but you know they're there. Clearly."

Suzy rolled her eyes.

"Studying about them and their conquests," she said, "I kept picturing *The Lord of the Rings*."

"Have I ever told you how much I love nerd girls?"

"But eventually," she continued, ignoring his remark, "my interest focused on the early American colonies, particularly New England. Whatever knowledge I have now of Native Americans deals primarily with Massachusetts tribes like the Wampanoag, the Narragansett, and others in that area."

"Well, as I recall, we didn't treat them very well, either."

Suzy sighed.

"Poor Birdsong," she said, getting back to their discussion. "She wants nothing more than to help her people, to be a lightworker, as you pointed out."

"You know, considering what we now know about her time period, she was probably one of the first lightworkers."

"But in the process, she's lost everything."

37

Birdsong watched her village from the cover of a stand of trees off the trail above. Her heart still ached from her earlier visit with White Wolf. She had spent the last couple of days wandering through the forest crying, partly for her own loss, but even more for the loss of all the families in the village.

She also missed Honeybee, White Wolf's sister. Having grown up together, they were like sisters themselves. She wondered why Honeybee hadn't sought her out, but she remembered that their mother was sick now with this illness. Honeybee would be busy caring for her.

As she looked over it, she noted that the village was eerily still. The men should be returning from their hunts now, the women beginning preparation of the evening meals. But aside from the guard posted at the north side of the village, visible from her vantage point, there was almost no activity.

She felt the grief and pain emanating from the camp, and it made her heart hurt.

Sitting there watching, her chin resting on her knees, a movement caught her eye. Somebody was backing out of a shelter. Noticing its position, she realized that it was the nest of White Wolf's family. She could see now that it was White Wolf himself who had backed out of the shelter, weighed down with a burden.

His mother, Moonlight.

White Wolf held her shoulders, as his father, Crow Feather, held her legs. She could just make out the grief-stricken expression on White Wolf's face as he straightened up, and Birdsong stood, clapping a hand over her mouth, the tears welling in her eyes.

They carried Moonlight through the camp toward the east side, toward their burial ground, but she lost sight of them before then. Even before she left the village a few days ago to consult the Old Spirits, their death rituals had been put aside, as there were just too many people dying in quick succession.

That weighed heavily on Birdsong's mind. Through her entire life, the dead were publicly mourned, their bodies decorated with ceremonial clothing and beads made of tusk and bone, buried in the ground with personal possessions. This aided them on their journey into the spirit world, helping them to make the transition more easily. It also demonstrated the love and devotion of the living for their dead loved ones.

What will the Old Spirits, and the new ones, for that matter, think of them for curtailing these ceremonies? What consequences will await her people, besides those already afflicting them? She understood the reason behind it, but it worried her.

In time, White Wolf returned, supporting his father, who seemed older and weaker than Birdsong had ever seen him. Before they got back to his shelter, Crow Feather stopped and bent over, hands on his knees, and cried. White Wolf helped him straighten up, and he put his arms around him, holding him up as the old man wept over his dead wife.

From White Wolf's position, his head was tilted to the side beside his father's. When he opened his eyes, he was looking up in Birdsong's direction. Birdsong could see the jolt of his body when he saw her. Crow Feather felt it, too, and he looked up at White Wolf's face.

Birdsong's first inclination was to duck behind the foliage that she had earlier hidden behind, but it was White Wolf. She loved him. And besides, he had already seen her. What would be the point of trying to hide?

Crow Feather looked up in the direction that White Wolf was looking, and when he saw Birdsong, his body started shaking, his grief giving way to the easier outlet of anger.

"You!" he shouted, pointing his finger up at her, his face contorted, his voice shaking. "You're the witch that killed my wife!"

"Crow Feather," Birdsong cried, "I'm not a witch, and I didn't kill Moonlight. I wanted to help her!"

The guard, looking up at her, seemed confused as his head pivoted between Birdsong and Crow Feather. He knew Birdsong, although she didn't know how much he knew about the village elders' decision concerning her. But he seemed content to allow her and Crow Feather to work it out, until further notice.

White Wolf tried to calm his father. Birdsong couldn't hear what White Wolf said to him, but the old man's shouts had already roused others. A few people came out of their nests, looking up the mountain when they saw White Wolf and Crow Feather.

Too late to hide now, Birdsong stood her ground, looking primarily at White Wolf, but her attention was diverted when she saw someone pushing his way through the people. Stone Face, a spear in his hand, his expression as hard as his name, looked up at her.

"You were warned to stay away from here," he shouted, pointing menacingly at her with the spear, his voice quivering with emotion. "You've learned your mother's magic well. You and your evil spirits are not welcome here."

"Stone Face," Birdsong implored, "the medicine I left with White Wolf could help our people. It was given to me by the Old Spirits." She thought it best, under the circumstances, to not mention her mother.

"We poured your medicine into the fire!" he replied with a sneer. "We can't lose any more of our people to your evil witchcraft!"

Birdsong's heart dropped when she heard that. A dark sense of hopelessness crept over her. Stone Face, perhaps noting her lapsed attention, drew back the spear and threw it as hard as he could in her direction.

His aim was good, the spear flying between the trees toward Birdsong. But the old man didn't have the strength for the trajectory needed to hurl the spear at such an upward angle to where she stood above them on the mountainside. Birdsong was startled out of her unhappy reverie when the spear clattered against the stones a few feet downhill from where she stood.

Jumping back, she looked down at the spear, then at the faces looking up toward her. She paid special attention to White Wolf's face. She just couldn't determine what he was thinking. His face seemed cold, angry, but how much of that was created by the lines of grief at the loss of his mother, and how much by the words of the village elder?

One thing she did notice, though, was the fact that he took a couple of steps away from his father, toward Stone Face, after he saw the elder throw the spear.

She hadn't lost him yet!

§

Birdsong retreated up the mountain toward her Spirit Circle to ponder what to do. Should she make more medicine, or would it be a futile effort? Would it just be poured into the fire like the last batch? Should she even stay here, or should she find a place to hide? She didn't know if Stone Face might follow through on his apparent attempt to kill her.

Given the fact that the elders had intruded in her Spirit Circle with no ill effects, it appeared that it would be no protection to her. Which made her begin to wonder if their conjecture was correct. Had the Old Spirits really abandoned her?

In the end, she decided to make more medicine, in case she did still have the Spirits' blessing, and in case the elders relented. She hoped that, while she was away, White Wolf would talk to them to sway their decision about her. Even if she wasn't accepted back into the village, she was sure that the medicine could help some of her people.

She spent the rest of the afternoon much like she had the day that she made the first batch, gathering the ingredients she needed, this time getting a couple of bee stings in the process. Fortunately, she didn't repeat the encounter with the mammoth.

Having dug up and eaten the last of the rabbit that she had killed, she had its skin in the Spirit Circle, along with the skin of the large chipmunk she had killed for breakfast the day before. She worked on hastily curing their skins to make a new waterskin to contain the medicine, once again chafing at the time it took to prepare them. She hoped that the rushed construction of it didn't adversely affect the waterskin or the medicine, but she felt that she didn't have a choice. The longer she spent in her preparations, the more people could die.

By the time she was finished, it was nearly morning. She picked up the odd waterskin, lopsided from its hasty construction, but so far, it was holding the medicine without leaking. When she was about halfway down the trail, she wished once again that she had thought to put her upper garment on. It had been warm by her fire, and with her fevered toils, but the night was chilly.

She crept down the mountain toward the village but, knowing it would have been too much to expect, she found that White Wolf was not on guard duty this time. By the light of the fire near the guard station, she saw that the man on duty was Tusk, Stone Face's younger son. Birdsong knew from experience that he could be counted on to always side with his father. She felt exasperated as she sat down to wait for the change of guard.

She thought about Red Flower, and other friends who had died in the past several days. Having time, but nothing to occupy her mind except her personal thoughts, the tears began to flow again.

Birdsong jerked awake, having dozed off, when she heard quiet voices down below. She looked to see who Tusk's relief was. It wasn't White Wolf.

She sighed and settled back against a tree to think. The dim light of early morning was approaching. The sun hadn't risen yet, but the scattered patches of sky she could see through the trees overhead were lightening a bit. It was still dark on the ground, but it wouldn't be for long. She needed to find White Wolf.

She picked up her bow, her quiver and the waterskin and, staying off the path, stealthily made her way down through the forest, choosing her steps carefully to be as quiet as possible. She hoped that White Wolf was in their nest, so she went there first. She stood outside, her ear turned toward the skin-covered hut, listening for any sounds from inside. There was nothing.

She ducked in through the door flap and cautiously felt around in the darkness. Her hands confirmed what her ears had told her. The shelter was empty. She lingered a few moments, remembering her last morning in here with White Wolf, his body against hers. So much had changed, in such a short time!

If White Wolf wasn't on guard duty, and he wasn't in their nest, then he must be staying with his father and sister, to comfort them in this time of loss.

She peeked out the flap to make sure nobody was around to see her. Then she came out, her bare feet stepping silently toward Crow Feather's nest. Though the sky was growing lighter, it was still quite dark in the shadows between the nests, and she picked her way carefully.

Standing outside, she paused to decide what to do. If she just quietly slipped in, she wouldn't be able to see once inside, unless they had a fire burning, and she didn't know where White Wolf would be sleeping. But if she tapped, she could wake Crow Feather, or Honeybee, White Wolf's sister.

As she stood there pondering what to do, she heard sounds of distress and a shuffling from inside. Her heart pounding, she took a deep breath and pulled back the flap, slipping inside.

By the glow of the embers of a small fire, both Crow Feather and White Wolf were kneeling beside Honeybee. They looked up at Birdsong, startled. Birdsong, her heart dropping in despair, saw Honeybee, her body still and grey. She saw the grief on the faces of White Wolf and his father, and the anger and hatred that appeared on Crow Feather's face when he saw Birdsong.

"The foreign witch has come back!" he said, his voice trembling, his tears tracing glistening streaks down his face.

"Crow Feather," Birdsong pleaded quietly, hoping to not draw the attention of the whole village, "you know me. I'm not a witch. I want to help."

"You've already taken my wife. Now you've taken my daughter, as well!"

White Wolf didn't seem to know what to do. Birdsong had hoped that he would speak up in her behalf, convince his father that she was telling the truth. Instead, he sat there looking down at his dead sister.

"I loved Honeybee as if she had been my own sister," Birdsong said as her own tears started to flow. "I would never dream of hurting her."

Crow Feather laboriously pushed himself up to face Birdsong. With his old back bowed as it was, they stood eye-to-eye.

"Get out of my nest," he said, his voice shaking. Birdsong looked tearfully down at White Wolf, who hadn't moved from Honeybee's side. "Get out!"

Birdsong jumped at Crow Feather's sudden shout, and she backed toward the door flap. Her lip quivering, she stooped out of the nest and straightened up, coming face-to-face with others who had apparently been alerted to her presence by Crow Feather's shouts. In front of them was Stone Face, a torch in one hand, his spear in the other.

"So," he said, "you persist in opposing our judgment."

"Stone Face," Birdsong said quietly, with all the respect she could muster, "I love my people. There is nothing that I want more than to help them. I've brought medicine that will help those who are sick."

"Everyone you have given your 'medicine' to has died. And still, you yourself are unaffected."

"You're wrong, Stone Face," she said, feeling a quiver of cautious defiance creeping into her voice, "I'm not unaffected. I am deeply *affected by the death and the suffering, the grief and the sadness of my people."*

"You're not affected by the sickness you are spreading here. You are protected by your evil magic while you separate us from the Old Spirits, making more of us sicken and die."

"I'm not making anybody die," she argued.

"You visited Storm Cloud and gave him your medicine," Stone Face retorted callously, "and he died. You gave Red Flower your medicine, and she died. You gave Tall Tree your medicine, and he died."

"She was here when Moonlight died," Crow Feather said behind her, and Birdsong turned to look at him, "watching from right up there on the mountainside. She didn't even have to use her medicine." The tears were still traversing his cheeks, shining in the torch light, and his voice cracked with emotion as he continued. "And she was just outside my nest now when Honeybee died." There was a collective gasp and sympathetic murmur from the growing crowd around them.

"So, you've taken another, have you?" Stone Face said coldly.

"I communed with the Spirits up there in the Spirit Circle," Birdsong said pleadingly, "so that I could make this new medicine." She grasped the waterskin and took it off her shoulder. "I care very much about all of my people. Nobody else has to die!" she cried.

"You keep speaking about your people," Stone Face sneered. "We have never been your people."

Birdsong felt that feeling again, the hurt of being excluded. But she tried to brush it aside, to speak through her tears.

"But so many of you have asked for my help. I've given it freely. I've wanted nothing but to help you."

"Where are those people now?" Stone Face asked. "They're dead."

"Snow," she said, gesturing toward a woman in front of her, "I've helped you many times with your stomach ailments. I've never harmed you, have I?"

Snow seemed embarrassed to be singled out, or afraid to be associated with an apparently dangerous person, and she shrunk back behind her husband.

"Lightning," Birdsong said, focusing on a couple of men in the crowd, "I mended your arm after that mammoth threw you against a rock. And River Ice, when the lion slashed your chest, I helped you recover."

Both men nodded a slight acknowledgment but, like Snow, acted as if they didn't want to be singled out.

"Friends have become enemies before," Stone Face said, "since the Old Spirits placed us on the earth."

"But I'm not an enemy!" Birdsong insisted, the tears flowing down her cheeks. "If you send me away, you will be left without a healer. What will you do?"

"We will not just send you away," Stone Face replied. "You have persisted in ignoring our judgment. And you have killed too many of us to just let you go free. Mortal enemies must be dealt with more severely than that."

As the first light of the sun shone through the trees on her skin, Birdsong shivered as his meaning became clear.

"You mean to kill your healer?" she asked quietly.

"Death will come," he said, "eventually. But it must be made clear to your evil spirits that we will not tolerate their representatives in our midst. It will be slow and painful. And then, when you are dead, you can tell your spirits that any witch they send among us in the future will be dealt with in the same way."

Birdsong shuddered as she looked at the cold hatred on his face, but she could think of no response.

"We will have a healer who is actually one of us," he continued coldly. "Someone we won't have to be suspicious of. Someone who won't curse us with evil magic." He focused on someone behind her. "Are you ready to take that responsibility?"

Birdsong turned and saw White Wolf approaching slowly from Crow Feather's nest. His face looked hard, lined with emotion, creased with fatigue and grief. When he saw Birdsong, she thought his face softened a bit, though she couldn't be sure. It was subtle and fleeting and, as if remembering his dead sister in the nest behind him, he looked back at Stone Face, his own face quickly clouding again.

"White Wolf," Birdsong said, "you believe me, don't you? I loved Honeybee. I love you." She turned and looked at those gathered around. "I love all my people."

"I believe you did," he said, turning his tired gaze back to her. "I believe you took your responsibility seriously in the beginning. But I believe that you were corrupted by the evil spirits and the new ideas that your mother introduced, and by allowing them in, you've endangered us all."

"White Wolf was trained by our old medicine man and will resume his work," Stone Face said.

"But that was such a long time ago," Birdsong protested quietly, brusquely wiping the tears away. "He has been helping me recently, but he doesn't have the experience he needs to fully serve the village."

"He has been appealing to the Old Spirits to recall the training to his mind," Stone Face replied with a cold smile. "And we have been entreating them in his behalf. He will serve as a fine medicine man," then his voice hardened again, "and without the contamination of your mother's evil magic." He looked at a couple of men near him. "Take her," he ordered.

Each man took her by an arm, holding on to her tightly, though she didn't struggle.

She looked at White Wolf, her breath stuck in her chest. With fresh tears balancing on her eyelids, she felt as if she couldn't exhale. "White Wolf," she finally whispered, "will you let them torture me to death?"

His face relaxed again, his expression softening as he looked at her. He struggled to hold on to his hard, stony countenance, but in the early morning sunlight, she could see the glassy look in his eyes as they filled with tears. His chest rose and fell with his conflicting emotions.

He reached out and took the spear from Stone Face's hand. Stone Face allowed him to take it, curious, likely hoping to see White Wolf's loyalty demonstrated. The spearhead was loose, the binding sinews frayed from clattering against the rocks the day before.

White Wolf's lower lip quivered slightly as he blinked the tears away, and they tumbled down his cheeks. Before Stone Face could stop him, he turned toward Birdsong.

She felt the spearhead tear into her body between her ribs just below her left breast, and she caught her breath in a moment of agonizing pain. The pain passed quickly, though, and a series of images registered in her eyes. White Wolf held her gaze for the briefest moment, and the pain showing in his eyes hurt Birdsong more than the physical pain she felt. She hoped he could see the gratitude she felt for at least sparing her from the torture.

White Wolf yanked the shaft of the spear away, the spearhead no longer attached to the end of it. Stone Face tried, too late, to stop him and snatched the naked spear shaft from his hand.

Birdsong felt her body grow heavy, and the grip of the men holding her wavered, as they didn't know whether to hold her up or let go of her. The color drained from the people in front of her as her vision faded. The golden light of the sunrise and the greenery of the forest that she had loved her whole life was the last thing she saw, before it became drab and lifeless, blurring into an aggregate of grey, finally fading to black.

40

Finn woke up when he thought he heard an unfamiliar sound. He reached beside him and found Suzy's side of the bed empty and cool. He sat up in bed, looking around his room in the early-morning grey. She wasn't anywhere around.

He heard the sound again, and he recognized it. Suzy was crying. He quickly got out of bed and pulled a robe on. Listening outside his door, he heard the sound coming up the stairs.

Fin pounded down the steps. Following the sound, he entered the living room, squinting to sharpen his vision in the predawn darkness. He saw a lump of something of a slightly different shade from the sofa, and it moved when he entered. He rushed to Suzy's side, placing his hand on her shoulder.

"Honey, what's wrong?" he asked softly. Suzy quickly sat up and threw her arms around Fin, choking him in the process.

"She's dead, Fin."

"Who?" he asked quietly, hesitantly, fearing some personal catastrophe.

"Birdsong."

"Oh, sweetheart," he said, trying to hide his sigh of relief. He settled on the sofa beside her, as Suzy loosened her grip around his neck. "We already knew that. She's been dead for twelve thousand years."

"I know," Suzy whimpered. "But now, I was there. I saw it. I *experienced* it!"

Fin sat back in the sofa, holding Suzy, letting her fill him in on the final episode of Birdsong's life.

"What a shit!" he said after she finished.

"Who?"

"White Wolf."

"He saved her from being tortured to death."

"He didn't save her," Fin protested. "He just killed her faster. I mean, it was *something* of a mercy, but he still killed her. Why didn't he stand up to Stone Face? It's like he wanted the power or prestige that Stone Face was offering him more than he wanted Birdsong."

"That's true," Suzy replied shakily.

"I'm surprised that didn't occur to you," Fin observed.

"I guess I still have Birdsong's thoughts and emotions muddled up with my own. Things were very different back then. Birdsong seems to have just accepted her fate, as if it was the will of the Spirits. I'm still kind of feeling that."

Holding Suzy in his arms, Fin noticed a glow upon them. He looked first toward the window, thinking the sun was rising, but the glow was coming from the doorway.

Suzy felt Fin stiffen, heard his sudden intake of breath, and she opened her eyes and looked up. Birdsong was standing there, watching them.

She looked much like she did when she was stalking Fin, her long black hair pulled back and tied with a strip of leather. She had full lips and almond-shaped eyes with epicanthic folds, much like Asian or Inuit eyelids. She wore an animal skin around her hips and carried her bow in her hand, but all her arrows, to Fin's great relief, were safely contained in the small quiver on her back.

She glowed softly with a blue-white light, surrounded by the shimmery aura that reminded them of heat on the embers of a fire. Seeing her now, without the animosity she had displayed before, Fin was able to relax a bit.

"You now know my life, and my death," she said softly. Only Suzy understood her.

"Yes, Birdsong," Suzy replied as the tears renewed. "I'm so sorry." Birdsong's face softened toward Suzy with a sad smile. "Do you know anything about what happened after you were killed?"

A crease formed between Birdsong's eyebrows as she frowned.

"I remember fragments of images," she said. "I was not buried in the burial ground. I did not deserve to rest with my people. Instead, Stone Face told the men holding my arms to pick up my body and throw it down the hillside, to be eaten by scavengers.

"I remember children happening by much later. I remember the look of disgust on their faces when they looked at what was left of my body.

"I remember the colors of the forest changing with the seasons around me, blankets of snow covering me in the winters, and new grasses and plants growing around me and through me.

"I remember when I no longer saw any of myself left on the ground, after the forest had consumed me. After that, I don't remember anything."

Suzy cast a hurried glance at Fin before she spoke, forgetting that he couldn't understand what they were saying.

"So, do you have any idea how long it's been since then?"

"No. I know it must have been many seasons."

Suzy sighed as she thought about how to respond.

"I can't tell you exactly how long it's been," Suzy paused, hoping the information wouldn't be too traumatic, "because your people didn't leave a written history. But we do know it's been somewhere around twelve thousand years."

Birdsong looked at Suzy for several moments, her face a blank. Suzy didn't know if Birdsong even had a way to comprehend that much time. She did some quick division in her head.

"That's something like two hundred lifetimes ago," she finally said. Birdsong's face still showed little reaction, and Suzy wondered if her people had even possessed any kind of numbering system.

"What will happen to me now?" Birdsong asked, apparently oblivious to the revelation.

"I don't know for certain," Suzy replied. "That's partly up to you. I may be able to help you move on to the next place." She noticed the confused look on Birdsong's face, so she clarified. "To join the Old Spirits." Birdsong nodded. "Or, if you prefer, we can return you to the mountain where you came from. We're going back up there tomorrow. That will be a long, lonely existence, but I don't want to influence your decision."

The relief on Birdsong's face was tangible.

"I would like to see my village again."

"Oh, honey," Suzy said with a sad, sympathetic tone, "your village isn't there anymore. It's been gone for - many seasons."

"I would like to see."

§

"What if we leave the spearhead on the mountain, and someone else finds it and takes it home with them?" Fin asked as they neared Silver Plume. "Someone who lacks your unique skillset?"

"We'll just have to bury it and cover the spot, disguise it so nobody else gets curious about it."

Fin nodded.

"It's a shame," he said after some time passed. "It's a beautiful artifact." He glanced at Suzy. "But you're right, Birdsong's happiness is more important."

Suzy smiled and put her hand on his.

Just like the first time they arrived, Jim Watkins, Dolores' father, was sitting on the front porch, and he got up and went inside when they parked. Dolores was waiting for them at the door when they walked in.

"It's so good to see you again," she smiled. "Welcome."

"Thank you," Fin and Suzy replied simultaneously.

"I have your paperwork all ready for you."

"After we get settled," Suzy said, as Fin signed the papers, "we'd like to talk to you for a few minutes, if you have the time."

"Okay," Dolores responded, a little mystified. "That'll be fine."

She led them up the steep, narrow stairway and stopped at a room right at the top of the stairs. Suzy glanced excitedly at Fin as Dolores unlocked the door.

"It's a small room," Dolores said with a bit of an apology in her voice, "but it was the only one available at this short notice. And it *is* a cozy one."

"Oh, it's fine," Fin said as she opened the door. "It's very nice."

Dolores smiled and gave him the key.

"Well, I'll be down in the kitchen whenever you want to talk." At that, she turned and went out the door, heading back down the stairs.

"What was that excited glance for?" Fin asked.

"This was Melody and Harmony's room!" Suzy replied enthusiastically. "I recognized its position at the top of the stairs. It's been updated. Obviously, they didn't have a bathroom then. And it's decorated much more nicely, but this is where they stayed when they arrived in town."

"Cool," Fin said, looking around apprehensively.

Suzy noticed his tone of voice sounded a little more nervous, a little less excited than hers.

§

Suzy was hanging a couple of things in the closet when she heard Fin's surprised voice.

"What are you doing in here?" He sounded startled. Suzy turned around and saw a pretty auburn-haired girl in a long, old-fashioned dress a few feet away.

"Melody!" Suzy said happily.

Fin looked at Suzy as the realization sunk in. It was the first time he had seen Melody. Standing there in the light of their room, he noticed that she looked like a normal, living person. This was just like Suzy had described Catriona, the little girl she had befriended in Scotland. In the daylight, she appeared substantial, corporeal, unlike the apparitions they witnessed in the dark, when their appearance resembled the shimmering waves of heat on the coals of a fire.

"I thought that was you!" Melody said.

"It's so good to see you again!" Suzy glanced over at Fin and reached for him, taking his arm. "Melody, this is my – my boyfriend, Fin. Fin," she leaned affectionately against him, "I'd like you to meet my friend, Melody Martin."

Despite his anxiety over once again being in the presence of an animated dead person, he couldn't help but crack a slight smile at Suzy's verbal stumble. It was the first time she had introduced him to anyone.

"Pleased to meet you," he said quietly. Melody actually curtsied.

"We're only here for tonight," Suzy said. "I'd love to see the rest of your story, if there's time."

"Are you sure?" Melody asked, a concerned look on her face. "I gave you a happy ending the last time you were here."

"Yes, but it wasn't really the end, was it?"

Melody gazed at her for a few moments, before acquiescing.

"You're right," she nodded, and her face relaxed into the smile that Suzy had become familiar with.

41

Cordelia, as relaxed and happy as Melody had ever seen her, nuzzled against Melody's neck. They were fully clothed but snuggled together on the settee in the parlor, with the curtains pulled under the excuse that it was warm and sunny outside, and they were keeping the heat out of the house. They were relaxed, more lying than sitting, but always alert to the sound of someone coming in the front door so that they could quickly regain their usual locations on each end of the settee.

Melody turned her head to face Cordelia, and Cordelia lifted her head to look into Melody's eyes. Since Harmony had moved out, Melody had spent several nights with Cordelia in her quarters, to make love and sleep in each other's arms, only slipping out and into her own room before the remaining boarders rose.

"I never thought I could feel so happy," Cordelia said, looking into Melody's eyes from inches away.

"I feel the same way," Melody replied breathily. "Considering that I lost my parents a year ago, and my sister just a couple of weeks ago, I'm amazed at how happy I am."

She pulled Cordelia close and kissed her, loving the feeling and the taste of her lips. She seemed to have gotten past the burning feelings of guilt that had kept her awake earlier. She still didn't know if she was going to burn in hell or not. But she had decided that she couldn't spend much time thinking or worrying about it. Cordelia was here and now, warm and soft in her arms. Every free moment, she reveled in Cordelia's love.

She still played at the Grizzly Bar with Harmony, but that was, now, strictly a business relationship. Harmony sang to her accompaniment but, under Taylor Tuttle's influence, Melody suspected, she insisted on more spirituals. Their audience, though, didn't seem to share her feelings, and often shouted out requests for more popular, secular tunes.

Melody's favorite times now were when she had moments like this to spend with Cordelia.

Cordelia ran her fingers through Melody's hair, pushing it back from her face. Gazing lovingly into her eyes, she smiled.

"I can't wait for you to meet Jesse next month," she said.

"Hmm," Melody replied, returning Cordelia's smile, "if he's anything like his mother, he must be adorable." Then, her face became serious. "He's three years old, right?" Cordelia nodded. "So he's going to be around all the time, for the next couple of years anyway." Even though nobody else was in the house, Melody whispered the next question. "How are you and I going to have any intimate time together?"

"Well," Cordelia replied slowly, as she put her thoughts in order, "I've been hoping that he'll be malleable enough that I can raise him to accept us as normal. At the same time, I hope to make him understand that that's not the way most people think, and that he needs to keep quiet about it." Melody raised an eyebrow in doubt. Cordelia nodded again. "I admit it may be rather precarious for a while."

"If he's anything like his mother, I'm sure he's also very smart," Melody said.

"Stop piling on the compliments," Cordelia blushed.

"I'm absolutely serious. You're the most intelligent woman I know. You're also a wonderful lover, a great friend, an amazing cook, and I can't imagine you being anything less than a good mother. Land sakes, Cordelia, I think you're almost perfect!"

"Oh, stop," Cordelia said, leaning forward against Melody. "I'm nowhere near perfect."

Melody flinched when she saw a man standing in the doorway of the parlor. She didn't recognize him, but as Cordelia turned, following her gaze, she stiffened. She pushed herself up against Melody's leg, choking on her breath.

"Lee!" she exclaimed. "I didn't hear you come in." She attempted to make her voice sound normal and unaffected, but didn't quite succeed.

"I came in through the back door," he said.

Remembering Cordelia's story of the beatings her husband had given her, and especially the last one, which left her with her scar and her limp, Melody was holding her breath. Physically, the man was a near match for Cordelia, his light skin and hair just a shade darker than hers.

His countenance, though, could not have been more different. His features were hard, his eyes were grey and cold, the sneer on his face deepening as he looked at Cordelia's hand still resting on Melody's thigh. With a rustle of the fabric of Melody's skirt, she self-consciously pushed herself up into a sitting position.

"Still engaged in your whorish abominations, I see," he said.

"Lee, what are you doing here?" Cordelia demanded.

"I needed some money," he said. "I was thinking it was time to put this house up for sale."

"You can't do that! This is my home!"

"Actually, it's still my *home," he replied, as he walked into the parlor. "But I reckon it's time to let it go."*

"I have boarders, Lee. And I live here."

"Not for long," he said, his voice chillingly quiet as he picked up the poker from in front of the fireplace.

"Lee, don't!" Cordelia said with a brittle voice, cracking despite her attempts to keep it firm. She pushed herself up on her cane.

"Got yourself a damn red-headed whore this time, huh? I suppose that's more fitting."

"Get out of here, Lee!"

He ignored her as he lifted the poker. Still standing near the fireplace, he was closer to Melody, and she became his first target. But Cordelia moved between them, instinctively turning her back to the blow. The poker cracked against her ribs, and she gasped at the pain, while Melody screamed, trying to push herself up, but Cordelia was in front of her, struggling to not topple over on her.

She reached for Cordelia, hoping to pull her back to the settee and away from Lee. All three of them heard the front door bang open against the wall, and Clifford Griffin appeared in the doorway of the parlor. He hadn't had the presence of mind to remove his bowler from his head, but he had a revolver in his hand.

"I heard you were back in town, Watkins," he panted, as if he had run all the way there.

"Griffin," Lee snarled. "God damn it, I knew I should have killed you back then instead of taking your payoff to leave town."

"Perhaps so," Griffin agreed. "Perhaps I should have been the one to kill you. Leave now and nobody has to get hurt."

"You're trespassing in my house, Griffin," Lee replied. "Why don't you leave, and I promise you won't be the one to get hurt." Without giving him the opportunity, though, he lifted the poker again, but instead of swinging it toward either of the women, he threw it across the room at Griffin.

It struck Griffin's hand just as he squeezed the trigger, giving him a painful bruise across his knuckles.

Melody felt a sudden pain in her abdomen, and everything went dark for a moment. When she opened her eyes again, scenes and sensations registered in her mind in a series of vignettes.

She saw Watkins struggling with Griffin in their mortal dance across the parlor.

She saw Cordelia sitting next to her on the settee, tightly gripping her cane as she watched the men grappling.

She heard the sound of the revolver firing, and she saw Watkins drop to the floor.

She saw Cordelia's face turn to her with relief, and then she saw the relief melt away and turn to fear and horror and sadness as Cordelia saw the scarlet stain spreading across Melody's dress.

She saw Griffin kneel before her, and the distress on his face as he realized that he had been the one who shot her.

She felt Cordelia grip her hand, heard her crying her name, and Melody squeezed Cordelia's hand just before everything in her view faded to black.

§

The vignettes continued later. Some of them included her own body which, to her chagrin, she could now see in front of her.

Griffin, his face drawn and somber, had Watkins' body removed from Cordelia's house, while frequently glancing toward Melody, where Cordelia was weeping pitifully over her body.

From the way Cordelia held and caressed Melody, and by the slightly disheveled condition of their clothing, he seemed to have figured out who it was that Melody had given her heart to.

Later, she saw Harmony come into the house, shadowed by her new husband, Taylor Tuttle, his hand protectively on her shoulder. By this time, Melody's body had been laid out and arranged on the settee, with a blanket pulled up over the scarlet stain.

Harmony choked when she saw Melody, sobbing and leaning against Tuttle, her hand clutched over her mouth. They didn't stay long, but when they left, Tuttle was still supporting Harmony.

Mr. Webb and Mr. Parker, as well as Miss Vincente, a new boarder, filed in as they arrived and paid their respects.

Griffin had left earlier in the evening, as others started coming in to see Melody and console Cordelia. His concert from the cliff was particularly somber that night. He finished with a slower-than-usual version of Mountain Melody, *as if holding on to it as long as he could. After that, the sound of a gunshot echoed down the valley.*

Townsfolk who rushed up the trail toward the mine and the cliff found his body there in a shallow grave he had, apparently, dug himself, the revolver still in his hand. A note nearby spoke of his profound grief, and asked that he be buried there.

The vignettes ended there, and Melody's story came to an end in darkness.

42

"That's quite a talent," Dolores said, though she seemed a little skeptical. "How long have you been able to do this?"

They were in the sitting room, Fin and Suzy in a loveseat, while Dolores sat in a chair opposite them.

"About a year and a half," Suzy replied. "It started with a ghost in my carriage house back home in Massachusetts, who turned out to be my great-great-great-great-great-grandmother. Since then, there have been a few more. But the reason I wanted to talk to you about it is that, well, I've made contact with a ghost here in your B&B."

Dolores' eyes opened wider, and her skepticism seemed to fly out the window.

"You've seen her?" she asked.

"I've seen her, spoken with her, and witnessed a portion of her life."

Dolores, dumbfounded, looked at Fin. He put up his hands and shook his head.

"I don't have that ability," he said, "though I have had a couple of somewhat unnerving encounters." Suzy smiled at his deliberate understatement.

"So, Dolores," Suzy said, "you asked if I've seen *her*. Can I assume that you've seen her yourself?"

"Well, I'm not sure," she replied a little breathlessly. "To be honest, there's been something of a family legend about it for as long as I can remember. A few guests have even reported seeing her, years ago. Some were scared, others thought it was fun. Anyway, I just figured they were people with overactive imaginations.

"But there have been times – well, you know that feeling that you're not alone? Sometimes, I had the feeling that someone was watching me. And once, I thought I saw someone at the top of the stairs when I knew nobody was here. But before I could focus, she was gone around the corner."

"What do you know about your great-grandmother?" Suzy asked. Dolores gasped.

"The ghost isn't her, is it?"

"No, I'm afraid not," Suzy smiled.

"You know, it's strange," Dolores said, "but I don't know a lot about my great-grandmother. She was a really private person. I know my great-grandfather was not a very nice man. He was known as something of a good-for-nothing. He beat her up a lot, and eventually, she killed him. Right in this very room, in fact. It was self-defense, of course. But she never did remarry."

"How did you choose the name 'Mountain Melody' for your B&B?" Fin asked.

"Ah," Dolores said, smiling wistfully, "that goes back to Clifford Griffin, the manager of the 7:30 mine. There was a young lady who lived here then, when this was a boarding house, run by my great-grandmother. The young lady's name was Melody Martin. There were rumors that Clifford Griffin took a shine to her.

"He made it a habit, every night, to play his violin at the top of the trail, on a cliff overlooking the valley. Supposedly, it could be heard down here in town. You hiked up there, if I remember right."

"Yes, we did," Suzy replied.

"We saw the grave marker at the top of the trail," Fin added.

"Yes, well, according to legend, his fiancée died back in New York just before they were to get married. He and his brother moved out here, but Clifford never got over her. He played his violin in a solo concert for her every night up on that cliff.

"But according to those rumors, Melody apparently caught his eye, and he composed a new song that he added to his repertoire, which somebody dubbed the Mountain Melody. I don't know if it's true or not, but I like to think that he found some happiness before he died.

"Unfortunately, my great-grandfather killed her just before he was killed himself."

"Well, Dolores," Suzy said, with an excited glance at Fin, "I have a surprise for you. The ghost in your B&B, the young lady you saw at the top of the stairs, is Melody Martin. She and her sister, Harmony, lived in the room that Fin and I are staying in now. I recognized it from the episodes of her life that I saw when we were here the first time."

"So you're telling me that my B&B really is haunted? It's not just legends or rumors or an overactive imagination?" Dolores asked, her eyes filling the lenses of her glasses.

"I don't think 'haunted' is the accurate word," Suzy replied. "That has a negative, scary connotation. Melody's such a sweet girl. I really like her. And Cordelia was very nice, too."

Dolores put her hand on her chest and sighed.

"You saw my great-grandmother?"

"I did. She was a very pretty woman, though she carried some scars from your great-grandfather. But - and this is why I asked what you knew about Cordelia - she had a very good reason for being such a private person, as you called her." Suzy paused, hoping to gauge Dolores' receptivity to the news. "She and Melody were in love with each other."

"Oh, my," Dolores said. "No, I never heard anything about that."

"I don't suppose so. As you might imagine, there was even less tolerance of homosexuality back then than there is now.

"But I have more news," Suzy continued with an excited smile, "and a gift for you. As it turns out, the rumor about the Mountain Melody *was* true. In one of Melody's later episodes, Clifford Griffin had written down the music and gave it to Melody. I followed the clues from those episodes and found where she hid it, in a cave outside of town." She picked up the yellowed oil silk envelope from her lap and handed it to Dolores. "We think it belongs here."

Dolores' eyes were engulfed in enormous tears behind her thick lenses as she took the envelope from Suzy. She gingerly opened it and pulled out four sheets of paper, two of them yellowed. The words 'Mountain Melody' were clearly visible at the top, in a lovely, not-quite-ornate, but carefully handwritten nineteenth-century script.

"We made copies of them," Fin said, "so you wouldn't have to keep handling the originals."

"Oh, my," Dolores said again. "I shall have to frame these," and she carefully set the originals aside on the side table. Then, she set about studying the music notation on the copies. Fin and Suzy sat there for a few moments, wondering if they should excuse themselves, until Dolores finally looked up at them.

"I don't know how to thank you both," she said. "I'm overwhelmed."

"You're welcome," Suzy replied. "It really is a beautiful song."

Dolores gasped again.

"And I'll bet you heard the original version, played by Clifford Griffin himself."

"I did," Suzy smiled. "He was very talented. I think you'll love it!"

Dolores stood up with the copies of the sheet music in her hands, but she hesitated and pointed toward the piano.

"Do you mind?" she asked.

"No, please," Fin replied. "Go ahead."

Dolores sat down in front of the piano and began playing. The melody was the same as Suzy remembered, both from the original violin solo that Clifford Griffin had played, and the version that Fin had played on his baby grand. But the brighter tone of the old upright piano, Suzy thought, gave it a sound more in keeping with the time period in which it originated.

Fin, being a lover of old things, also appreciated the difference in the sound from when he played it himself in his hobby room. Dolores was a more skilled player than he was, and played it well her first time through.

"This is so familiar," Dolores said.

Fin felt a sudden chill, and a movement to the side caught his eye. Turning to look, he jumped, surprised to see the same pretty auburn-haired girl he had seen in their room earlier, wearing the same long, old-fashioned dress, her hands placed across each other on her chest, as she listened to Dolores play.

Dolores and Suzy both noticed his gasp and turned to see what he saw. Dolores abruptly stopped playing. Suzy was the only one to speak.

"Melody!" she said, happily. "I'm so glad you decided to join us."

"Oh, my goodness!" Dolores exclaimed, standing up and clapping her hands over her chest, mirroring Melody's position. "You're Melody Martin?"

Melody nodded, with what appeared to be tears in her eyes.

"Land sakes, please don't stop," she said. "I haven't heard that in so long!"

Dolores, though, couldn't seem to turn away. Her eyes completely filling up the thick lenses of her glasses, she kept staring at Melody.

"Melody," she said, "I'm so happy to finally meet you! I'm Cordelia's great-granddaughter."

"I know," Melody said softly, smiling and slanting her head to the side a bit. "I've been here, watching her family since then. Don't you remember me?"

"What do you mean?" Dolores asked, scrunching her eyebrows together.

"I played with you when you were a little girl. And I taught you that basic melody on the piano, as I remembered it."

"Land sakes!" Dolores exclaimed, plopping back down on the piano stool.

§

After a few minutes, Dolores was able to turn back to the piano and play *Mountain Melody* again, smiling as she remembered the tune from her childhood. After she finished playing it through, the three of them turned to see Melody's reaction, but she was gone.

Suzy and Fin sat with Dolores for a few hours while Suzy related Melody's story to her in a little more detail. Though they were hoping to get an early start in the morning with taking Birdsong into the forest, they went up to their room later than they had planned.

The room was cold. They found Melody in there waiting for them.

"Land sakes!" she said, pointing excitedly. "Where did she come from?"

Suzy and Fin turned to see Birdsong, an arrow pulled taut on her bow, watching Melody warily.

"Birdsong!" Melody said in Birdsong's language. "It's alright. This is Melody. She's a friend."

"Why is she here?" Birdsong asked.

"This is where she used to live, a long time ago. Well, not nearly as long ago as you, but in this nest."

"Nest?" Melody asked. "That's an odd thing to call a house."

Suzy looked at her in surprise.

"You can understand us?"

"Sure. You're speaking English, aren't you?"

Suzy looked at Fin. He raised his eyebrows and shook his head.

"What?" he asked.

"Can you understand us?"

"I can understand you and Melody."

"Very interesting!" Suzy said, a smile creeping across her face. "Apparently, spirits of the dead can understand each other, even if they spoke different languages before they died."

"Why is she naked?" Melody asked. Then, her eyes flew open wide. "Is she a wild Indian? Clifford spoke about the Indians, but I never got to see any." She smiled at the memory.

Birdsong, confused, relaxed her bow but remained cautious.

"Well, no, not exactly," Suzy replied. "She was here a long time before the Indians of your time. She lived in this area about twelve thousand years ago. She wants to see where her village was, before she moves on to the next place."

Melody looked at Birdsong a little wistfully.

"She wants to 'move on,' as you call it?"

"She's not sure, but she wants to see the forest again. She misses it."

"I do, too," Melody confessed. "I used to love walking in the forest with Cordelia. Well," she suddenly blushed a little as she looked at Suzy, "I suppose you know that."

Suzy looked at Birdsong. She was now holding her bow down at her side, and the arrow was back in the quiver. In fact, Suzy could see what looked like tears in her eyes.

"You walked in the forest with someone you loved?" Birdsong asked.

"Yes!" Melody replied ardently. "Whenever we could."

"Then, you know the magic," Birdsong smiled sympathetically.

"Land sakes, I sure do!" Melody nodded, smiling, phantom tears in her own eyes.

43

After they got Melody and Birdsong calmed down, and managed to convince them to go wherever it is that they go when they're not 'present,' so that Suzy and Fin could have a little privacy, they finally went to bed. They woke up quite a bit later than they had planned.

They had hoped to be the first ones down for breakfast. They didn't want to linger, visiting with Dolores, who didn't know about Birdsong and explaining their plans for the morning, but they wanted to get an early start. As it was, they were the last ones down of all the guests.

Dolores smiled warmly at them when they appeared in the dining room, but made no mention of their visit with Melody the previous night. They took their seats at a table with another couple on the other end. They managed to keep the conversation to general information and pleasantries while they ate, but it was nearly 10:00 when they finally finished and went back upstairs.

Their packing was prolonged when Melody made another appearance.

"Should I 'move on'?" she asked abruptly, emphasizing the words 'move on.' "Will my sister and my parents be there?" Her voice took on a softened tone. "Will Cordelia be there?"

"Honey," Suzy replied, "I can't tell you that. I don't know how the afterlife works. I've never been there. And it's not up to me to tell you if you *should* move on to the next plane. That's for you to decide.

"I *can* say this: you do seem happier in this world than other spirits I've encountered. And you don't threaten or interfere with the lives of those in this world.

"At the same time, I remember you also expressed dismay that sometimes people are frightened when they see you. And you don't have anybody of your own kind to interact with here."

Melody stiffened her arms and shook her fists down at her side in a gesture of frustration.

"That doesn't help at all!" she said.

"I'm sorry," Suzy said, shaking her head.

"Do you mind if I interject something?" Fin asked shakily, trying to keep his breath steady. Both women, living and dead, looked at him with open expressions. "Melody, you're a very sweet young lady. From what Suzy has told me about your life, it just seems to me to be a shame for you to stay cooped up here as a ghost, where you can't be a bright and positive influence on others. You have too much joy and light to stay confined in this little area where others don't have the opportunity to get to know you."

He looked back and forth at both of them, and was momentarily distracted from his message to Melody by the look of overflowing love on Suzy's face.

"Land sakes, Fin!" Melody exclaimed. "If I wasn't dead, I'd –" Her apparition gave the appearance of a blush. "Well, just never mind what I'd do."

Fin, more befuddled than he ever remembered being, managed a smile combined with a shudder that made Suzy chuckle at his discomfiture.

"So, how do I go about 'moving on'?" Melody asked.

"Well," Suzy sighed, "from what I understand, there's something like a portal or a door with a light on the other side. If you look around where you are, you should see it, or be aware of it. Apparently, all you have to do is go towards it."

Melody looked squarely at Suzy and exhaled through her nose, her lips tightly pressed together. Seeing her youthful exuberance and ardor, Suzy remembered that Melody was only twenty-one when she died.

"Alright," Melody said, "I'm going to do it."

"Please be absolutely certain," Suzy urged her. "As far as I know, it's a one-way trip. Most likely, you won't be able to come back."

"Yes, I'm sure," Melody replied firmly. "But first, I must bid farewell to Dolores."

"I think that's a good idea."

"Well, by the time you get back, I suppose I'll be gone."

"We won't be back," Suzy said. "We were only here for one night this time." Melody looked at their luggage on the bed.

"Oh, so you're leaving, too?"

"Yes," Fin said, "we need to take Birdsong up the mountain." He glanced at the clock on the bedside table. "And we're already past checkout time." He raised his eyebrows at Suzy. "We should get going."

Suzy nodded and turned back toward Melody.

"Melody, it was wonderful getting to know you and to see what your life was like. I'm sorry it ended the way it did, but I hope that you find happiness in the next place."

"Thank you, Suzy. It was very nice spending a little time with someone who didn't run screaming from me." Melody smiled and looked at Fin. "I wish I could have known you better, but from what I've seen and heard, you two are made for each other."

"See?" Fin said, looking at Suzy. "What did I tell you? We're MFEO!"

"Best of luck to you, Melody," Suzy said, ignoring Fin's comment, to his chagrin.

"And to both of you," Melody said, as she smiled and faded away.

§

Like before, Fin found Silver Street and drove up the steep hill, parking at the trailhead. They got out of the car, Suzy carrying the spearhead in her hands. Knowing now that Birdsong was somehow connected to it, they didn't feel right just toting it up the mountain in Fin's pocket.

With a glance at each other, they started up the 7:30 mine trail. Almost an hour later, they arrived at their destination, the starting point for Birdsong's search.

"Here it is," Fin said, spotting the rock that they had rested on the first time, and where he had found the spearhead. He sat down on it to rest.

Suzy nodded and pressed her hands together protectively against the spearhead.

"Birdsong," she said in Birdsong's language, "we're here." They waited and didn't receive a response. As they looked around, they found Birdsong standing behind them. She was gazing around, her eyebrows drawn together.

"I don't recognize this area," she replied. She looked down into the valley and saw the little town of Silver Plume sprawled there among the trees, with I-70 rushing past in both directions just beyond.

She lifted her eyes beyond, and she stopped, tilting her head slightly.

"What is it?" Fin asked.

Before Suzy could respond, they heard footsteps approaching up the trail, and Fin fought back a sudden feeling of panic. He jumped to his feet as a couple of other hikers came around a bend. What would they think, seeing him with two women, one of whom was wearing nothing but an animal skin tied around her hips and a quiver of arrows on her back, a hunting bow in her hand?

His heart pounded as they came closer, and he racked his brain for a possible explanation to give, one that wasn't embarrassing, and one that didn't involve a twelve-thousand-year-old dead woman. He glanced at Suzy who, he thought, seemed somewhat concerned as well.

The hikers were nearly abreast of them now, and Fin flushed a bit as that particular word came to mind. He smiled nervously and, he knew, guiltily, as they passed, their feet crunching on the gravel.

"Good afternoon," they said. Suddenly, both hikers shivered as they walked past, just inches away from Birdsong.

Fin and Suzy both mumbled a greeting to them, and looked at each other.

"They didn't see her!" Fin said as they disappeared ahead of them, his voice dripping with relief.

"Apparently not," Suzy smiled. She sighed, seemingly relieved as well.

"Wow," Fin said, "I feel so special."

"What do you mean?"

"Well, I didn't see that little girl in Scotland, Catriona, until she appeared in her 'phantom state' with the other ghosts that night in the vaults. I've never seen the ghosts you see in your dreams. I've never seen any of the waking visions you see of their lives. The fact that Birdsong is allowing me to see her now, but not allowing others, just makes me feel like she trusts me or something."

"You saw Melody."

"That's true," Fin nodded, thinking. "But so did Dolores. And Melody is separated from us by less than a century and a half. That seems like a long time, but compared to twelve millennia, it's practically nothing. I don't know, it just feels kind of special."

"And her bare legs and breasts have nothing to do with you feeling special?" Suzy asked with a skeptical grin.

"Well," Fin responded with raised eyebrows, looking back at Birdsong, "there is that."

Suzy took his face in her hand and turned it back to look at her.

"You *are* special to me," she said. Fin smiled at her and kissed her. He rubbed his face as if to wake up, and he looked at Suzy.

"So, what's the plan?"

Suzy turned to Birdsong, who was still studying the landscape on the other side of Silver Plume.

"What do you see, Birdsong?" she asked in her language.

Birdsong, the spell momentarily broken, turned and looked at Suzy.

"Those hills," she said, pointing across I-70. "The shapes are familiar. I think I can find it now."

"Oh, that's good news!" Suzy turned to Fin and switched to English. "Birdsong said she recognizes the shape of those hills across the valley. She thinks she can find the location of her village now."

"Cool!"

Suzy looked at Birdsong. "Lead the way."

§

"So, what do you suppose her range is?" Fin asked as he watched Birdsong gliding through the forest several yards ahead of them.

Unlike when they saw her in her vaporous state, at night, she appeared to actually be walking, instead of just floating over the surface of the ground. Still, her movements were fluid and graceful, like an athletic hunter on the prowl. Suzy looked at him and smiled.

"You talk as if this spearhead is a modem and Birdsong is Wi-Fi."

Fin shrugged.

"I'm just curious. I know she's connected in some intangible way to the spearhead, but she can move that far away from it. I wonder what the limit is. And what happens if she tries to go beyond it?"

"No idea," Suzy replied. "I know she was able to appear to us downstairs when the spearhead was in the display case in your hobby room."

"That's true," Fin nodded, his face still contorted in thought, "but was the distance measured through the door of the hobby room, down the stairs, down the hallway, and through the doorway into the living room, or was it a more direct route right through the ceiling?"

Suzy looked at him for a moment as they trudged on through the forest.

"I can't believe I'm actually telling someone this, but you need to stop thinking so much!" Fin just grinned in response. "How long has it been?"

Fin checked the time.

"Damn, it's almost five o'clock," he replied. "No wonder I'm hungry! Do you think we're close yet?"

"I don't know. I sure hope so. Considering how far back you found the spearhead, I can't imagine the village, and the location where she was killed, being this far away from it. It seems as if we've walked several miles."

"Yeah," Fin said, "but I think we've zig-zagged up the mountain quite a bit since we left the trail. Remember what Professor Windsor said, about erosion bringing the spearhead to the surface. When we hiked the length of the trail last time, we saw evidence of landslides. I would think that rocks tumbling down the mountain can move stuff around quite a bit."

"I guess so." Suzy tried to catch her breath as she looked at Birdsong examining the terrain for anything recognizable. She sighed. "Still, I'm not feeling very keen about spending the night on this mountain." She looked ahead at the prehistoric huntress. "Birdsong," she called.

In an instant, Birdsong had turned and was standing directly in front of them. Fin and Suzy both recoiled a bit.

"Yes?" Birdsong inquired.

"Whoa!" Suzy said, clapping a hand over her chest as she gasped in surprise. She exhaled, then addressed Birdsong in her language. "Is anything looking familiar yet?"

"Not yet," Birdsong replied. "The forest looks so different from my –"

She abruptly stopped speaking and drew in a sharp breath as she spied something over Suzy's shoulder. Suzy and Fin both turned to see what had caught her eye. Through the trees, they saw what looked like a large chunk of granite, four or five feet wide and about six feet tall, jutting out of the ground, several yards up the hill from them.

"I didn't see that before," Birdsong said breathlessly. She started moving toward the boulder.

"You mean that rock?" Suzy asked as they struggled to climb the rough terrain after her.

"Yes," Birdsong replied. "The forest has changed, and even the stone seems a little different, but that's definitely it."

Even as she spoke, Suzy recognized from her episodes what had captured Birdsong's attention. It was the rock where Birdsong and White Wolf would meet for their forest liaisons. As they climbed the hill toward it, Suzy could see that Birdsong was right. It looked a little different, a few of the sharper angles rounded off, and a few more cracks, no doubt the result of twelve thousand years of weather and wear and tear.

Suzy knew they were close. The village was only a few hundred yards away.

Birdsong stood before the rock now, gazing intently at it, phantom tears standing on her eyelids. Suzy's reaction was similar, feeling the resurgence of the emotions that she had felt when the episodes involved Birdsong and White Wolf meeting, and especially, making love near the stone. Suzy felt a tingling sensation as she stood in front of the boulder. She really hoped Fin didn't ask her how she felt.

"The village was over here," she said, dragging herself out of her mental haze. She turned toward the east, and Birdsong followed, feeling torn, a little reluctant to leave the stone, and yet eager to see her village again. Fin fell in behind.

As they walked through the scrub and old aspen leaves and pine needles littering the ground among the trees, they were nearing the place where Suzy knew the village had once been. But there was no clearing now. As Suzy expected, there was no trace of the village, the area now thickly forested.

Birdsong looked around, her face indecipherable to Fin, though Suzy had an inkling of what she was feeling. Having shared Birdsong's emotions and experiences in the episodes she had seen, she felt sadness and loss. She had known that there would be no vestiges left of the village, but still, she felt the absence of the people, even after twelve thousand years.

Fin, oblivious to their dark thoughts and feelings, just followed along, looking around, and trying to visualize the prehistoric village that Suzy had described to him.

The slope of the mountainside leveled out, and even without having seen the episodes himself, Fin could tell that they had entered the area where, eons ago, a prehistoric village had once stood. He watched the women walking ahead of him, and he could see that they both seemed to be in a particularly poignant mood as they entered the area where Birdsong's people had once lived.

He also noticed something else. As the sun neared the high horizon of the mountains to the west, hidden to them in the dense forest, and the remaining sunlight had to filter through more trees, the light was fading in the woods. As darkness began settling around them, he could see the beginnings of that rippling effect on Birdsong's skin as her 'aura' became visible. Fin started feeling a little uneasy as Birdsong began looking less corporeal and more like a ghost.

"Easy," he thought, remembering his resolve to be less 'wimpy' about Suzy's ghosts. "Birdsong is just a kind soul who got a bad rap and met an untimely end," he told himself. A thought occurred to him that made him shudder, but he continued silently talking himself through it. "True, she would have skewered me with one of her arrows a couple of nights ago, but that was just the fear talking."

He stopped for a moment and let that thought simmer in his mind. Birdsong was afraid. She was a ghost, something that others generally find scary, yet *she* was afraid. She had been killed eons ago and woke up in a strange, unfamiliar world, completely alone, at least where her own kind were concerned. That would make anyone afraid.

Fin felt as if his fear was beginning to morph into something more like empathy. Putting himself in her position, he could understand her feelings. The writer in him examined these feelings, knowing it would help him when it came time to write the characters and the story that was unfolding before him.

He was suddenly yanked out of his reverie when Suzy gasped. He rushed to her side.

"What is it?" he asked, but before he even finished his question, he could feel what had caused her reaction. In this area, the air felt at least twenty degrees colder. In the deepening twilight, they could see their breath hanging in little white clouds in front of them.

Remembering the vaults in Edinburgh last year, and the first appearance of Birdsong in his bedroom a couple of nights ago, Fin knew what that ominous drop in temperature meant.

Birdsong was beside them now, and she seemed apprehensive. She reminded Fin of when he first saw her stalking her in his house, her face on alert, her body tense and in a slight crouch, as if ready for action. She was gripping her bow tightly, though she hadn't fitted an arrow to it yet.

Fin wasn't sure where to look, so he watched Suzy and Birdsong. In the dimming light, they both seemed focused on one particular pine, and he turned his attention to it. As he watched, it looked like the tree started smoking, as if from a smoldering fire within. The smoke seeped out through the scaly bark, but unlike smoke, it didn't rise and dissipate in the air. Instead, it coalesced in front of them, taking shape into a body that, based on the animal skin clothing, appeared contemporaneous to Birdsong.

As the wisps of smoke visually solidified, the features became clear, turning into the shimmering ember form that had become familiar to Fin and Suzy. When the facial features became apparent, both women emitted a sound as if they had choked on a breath.

"Stone Face!" they exclaimed. Fin made a similar sound when he realized that he understood what they said.

§

The elder, older than he appeared when the women had last seen him, looked at the three of them. His arms and legs were gnarled with age, his back bent. Instead of the spear he carried in Suzy's episodes, he now leaned on a staff. His face was still stern and angry-looking.

In keeping with the grotesque faces of the evil spirits she had seen the year before in Edinburgh and in her carriage house, Suzy noticed that Stone Face's features seemed sharper, more angular. But after all the ghosts she had seen and interacted with, she still didn't know if the appearance of the ghost was an accurate representation of the living person, and how much choice, if any, they had in this depiction.

Before she could put much thought into it, though, she was alarmed to feel the beginnings of an episode coming on. As she had at other times in the past, her mind was apparently picking up Stone Face's thoughts and, unable to stop it now that it had started, she wavered on her feet as her vision blurred.

Fin, seeing her body jolted and unbalanced, grabbed her, helping to support her, while Birdsong watched in shock. She turned back toward Stone Face, an arrow now fitted to her bow string, but Fin shouted at her.

"Birdsong, no!" Holding Suzy up with one arm, he put up his other hand in the universal 'stop' gesture, hoping that it was as universal in her day as it was now. "I don't know what would happen to Suzy if you forcefully break her connection to Stone Face."

Birdsong was surprised to understand him, and she also recognized his gesture, and the fear in his voice. She looked back at Stone Face who was scowling at the three of them. He seemed particularly flustered by Suzy, and Birdsong relaxed her bowstring, recognizing that whatever was wrong with Suzy probably wasn't his fault.

Which just made Birdsong that much more confused by what was happening to her.

§

Suzy couldn't fight the images flowing into her brain. She saw the village, though its appearance was somehow different than what she had seen in Birdsong's episodes. Shapes and proportions seemed a little off, colors were darker and more saturated, everything was skewed at awkward angles.

And the people seemed odd, as well. Facial features looked almost like cubist portraits, although she didn't have that reference available to her when she was actually in the midst of the episode. Faces were just twisted into grotesque images.

The scenes switched rapidly, not so much a chronological narrative, but more like hallucinogenic impressions. Included among them were a giant eagle, a saber-toothed cat, and a mammoth which, unknown to Suzy, caused her body to shudder when she saw it. These images were distorted, as well, the eagle's beak larger and sharper, the mammoth's tusks of an impossibly enormous girth, the saber-tooth's fangs at least two feet long, and razor-sharp.

There were more people, none of whom Suzy recognized for certain, likely due to the facial distortions of the vision. Besides those distortions, there were also rashes and mucous and blood seepage. In the next image, all the people in the scene were on the ground, some writhing in discomfort, others ominously still.

The next image she saw consisted of shadows, silhouettes of people, but with no details or features. There were old footprints on the ground, but no feet making new ones. The strange, skewed nests of the village were quiet, the door flaps blowing in the breeze, the forest casting dark shadows over them.

There were multiple images of trees and clouds and birds flying toward the sunset. There was the image of a jagged stone knife being held, based on her visual reference, in her own, gnarled hands, and she watched it as it moved down toward her chest. There was a moment of hesitation, then the knife plunged between her ribs, the resulting pain causing a visual discord of color and static and blurring, until everything went black.

§

Fin felt Suzy jerk, and he struggled with her weight as she suddenly collapsed in his arms.

"Oh my god!" he exclaimed, easing her down onto the pine needles and leaf litter on the ground. "Suzy!" He tried to revive her, shaking her shoulders, patting her cheeks, but she was out cold. "What did you do to her?" he yelled at Stone Face.

Stone Face looked down indifferently at Suzy, his usual scowl tinged with bewilderment about Suzy's condition, and he sneered at Fin. Fin, despite his fear, stood up and squarely faced him.

"Get the fuck out of here!" he shouted. Stone Face, like Birdsong, was surprised to understand him now. He smiled coldly, and his body began glowing more fiercely. The shimmering ember effect enveloping his body intensified and turned into flames, but before he had the chance to be any more threatening, Birdsong let loose her arrow. Not surprisingly, the arrow flew directly through Stone Face's body and dissipated into a wisp of smoke on the other side.

Stone Face barely reacted, as if a mosquito had tried to knock him down. He simply laughed derisively at her.

"You're so weak, Birdsong," he said. "And yet you were so arrogant," he pointed at her, "as to claim to have the blessing of the Old Spirits." As he jabbed his finger at her, whether by design or simply by a Newtonian law of motion, some of the flame sloughed off his arm and was flung toward Birdsong. Without thinking, Birdsong reacted and seemed surprised when her own shimmering embers turned into flames, providing an opposing force to Stone Face's flare.

Fin took a breath to try to calm himself. Remembering the ghost expulsions that he and Suzy had been involved in at

Edinburgh and Marblehead, he attempted to make a more dispassionate request of Stone Face.

"Stone Face, you can go through the door, into the light. You can move on to the next place." Fin was impressed with how calm he was. He didn't shout, but still, his voice was firm and authoritative.

Stone Face just looked at him blankly for a moment, pondering his words and authoritative tone. Then, as if considering himself the only authority present, he made a motion that resembled sucking a deep breath into his lungs, and as he did so, the flames covering his body glowed brighter and flared higher.

Birdsong quickly positioned herself in front of Fin and Suzy, hoping to protect them. As Stone Face started flinging flames at them, Fin threw himself over Suzy, while Birdsong attempted to repel the elder's assault.

Being unfamiliar with her abilities, though, Birdsong's results were paltry, being little more than showers of sparks flung in random directions. Stone Face laughed at her again and, spurred on by her obvious lack of experience, erupted into a ghostly inferno.

Fin felt the air around him pressurize, as it had in the vaults and in Suzy's carriage house. He was surprised to feel it out in the open air, unencumbered by walls, but he felt the unmistakable sensation of the air pressing against his body, making it difficult to take a breath.

He shivered, for while the air in front of him was hot, the air behind him was still quite cold, causing a sharp contrast. A deep hum filled the air, shaking the foliage on the trees above them, and Fin suddenly felt nauseated. As the pressure around him increased, he felt pain behind his eyes, and his head began pounding.

Birdsong steeled herself for Stone Face's attack, afraid that she didn't know how to fight him. When Stone Face hurled a ball of fire at her, it knocked her off balance, and she fell backwards across Fin and Suzy.

Fin shuddered as he saw Birdsong's face pass through Suzy's, then rise up out of it as she picked herself up. His shudder was quickly followed by relief, though, as Suzy stirred. She opened her eyes, blinking a few times. Looking at Fin, inches away, she frowned in confusion. As she saw what was happening, she rolled her eyes, and Fin almost grinned knowingly as he helped her to her feet.

Swaying unsteadily, supported by Fin, she looked at Stone Face, blazing on the other side of Birdsong, and she managed to pull a breath into her lungs.

"Stone Face," she shouted in the prehistoric language, "you need to move on and join your spirits."

The elder's flames faltered a bit when he was surprised to understand her, as well. But then he laughed at her puny attempt to control him, the flames climbing even higher than before, and pressing outward. Suzy and Fin tried to stand firm against the fiery onslaught, but the flames were threatening to engulf them, the hot wind burning their faces, while their hair and clothing waved wildly in the swirling maelstrom of hot and frosty air.

Just as the flames threatened to envelope them, the three of them saw a long, slender cloud of smoke flying through the forest toward them, coming up behind Stone Face. While preparing for Stone Face's attack, they were curious as the smoke encircled the elder. The stream of smoke rose and fell around him, continually flowing in an accelerating spiral, gradually drawing in tighter. Despite his efforts, his flames dissipated harmlessly into the air above him, as if out of a smokestack.

Birdsong glanced at Suzy. In that moment, Suzy nodded at her, and at Fin, and they all leaned forward and started shouting at Stone Face.

"Stone Face, you have to go!"

"Go and join the Spirits!"

"Move toward the light near you!"

"Go to the next place and leave us alone!"

"Get the hell out of here, you fucking monster!"

The latter was one of Fin's contributions.

With the combined opposition of the three of them, along with the tornadic cloud frustrating and weakening him, Stone Face finally seemed to give up. His flames extinguished and the man stood there looking weakly at them for a few moments from the midst of the smoking cyclone.

Finally, with an embittered shake of his head, the man vanished in a blinding flash of white light. The smoke that had encircled him, for the briefest moment, collapsed into a small point of light before exploding around them. It looked to Fin like a miniaturized reenactment of the singularity, billions of years ago, right before the Big Bang blew it outward in all directions.

Leaning forward against Stone Face's attack as they were, Suzy and Fin had to brace themselves as they were drawn momentarily toward the sudden vacuum. Just as quickly, though, the atmosphere around them equalized, and the smoke that had scattered began reassembling itself.

As the wisps were coming together, Fin was reminded of the liquid metal T-1000.

"Oh my god," he said, "it's the Terminator putting itself back together."

Suzy, panting for breath after her exertions, ignored his prediction and watched as the smoke did indeed congeal into a human figure, though it wasn't a futuristic machine.

"Honeybee!" Birdsong exclaimed.

§

After Honeybee had dramatically made her appearance, the two spirits had briefly discorporated and swirled together in what Suzy took to be something like an afterlife hug. Afterwards, having resumed their corporeal appearance, Honeybee was explaining why she was there.

"I discovered just after I died that I was not afraid. There were others here, including my mother, who were sad and frightened at the knowledge that we had died. But I was calm, and I found that I was able to help them. The light was there, and I was drawn to it, but others were afraid of it. I knew, somehow, that it's where we were supposed to go. But some had gone into the light and had not come back, and that frightened those who remained.

"I found that I had the ability to move back and forth between this place and the light, and I became convinced that it was my duty, my assignment to help others who were afraid. I could calm their fears and help them to 'move on,' as you call it, Suzy."

She looked at Birdsong.

"After you were killed," she said, "people in the village kept getting sick. White Wolf seemed distraught about killing you, but he kept his mind focused on working hard to try to help the sick. He asked Stone Face for the medicine that you had made, but Stone Face poured it out, like he had the first batch.

"Then, White Wolf got sick. After that, when nobody was able to help them, the illness spread even more quickly through the village.

"White Wolf died a few days after you. In time, everybody in the village died except Stone Face. He seemed, at first, proud of being so strong, or so blessed by the Spirits. But after several days, he recognized that he was all alone, and it started to affect his mind."

"He must have had some kind of immunity," Fin whispered to Suzy. Suzy nodded.

"He had dragged the rest of the bodies in the village to the burial ground, though he was not able to bury them all. He wandered from nest to nest. I don't know if he was looking for survivors, or for things they had left that he wanted for himself.

"I could tell that his mind was getting sick, and I tried to contact him. Sometimes it seemed as if he could hear me or see me, but he would shake his head and ignore me as if I was just a voice in his head.

"He lasted almost a year, though he aged quickly, raging at the trees, cursing the Old Spirits for leaving him here. Finally, though, his madness overwhelmed him and he killed himself.

"Even then, he would not listen to me. His anger had turned to hatred, and he held on to that madness as if it was a prized possession. He acted out his anger and hatred in many ways toward people who came later, showing himself as a great and vengeful spirit."

"Those Indian legends I mentioned earlier!" Fin said excitedly. "It really was a spirit. Just not a very nice one." Suzy nodded again.

"Stone Face was the last one of our people to go, but I decided that it was up to me to stay here," she smiled, "to try to be a good influence on him. I worked to keep him in line and prevent him from acting out too much, and from harming others.

"I had no idea you were still here," she said to Birdsong. "I was certain you must have gone into the light and had already joined the Spirits."

Birdsong had phantom tears standing on her eyelids as she listened to her friend.

"But now that Stone Face has moved on, and you're here, we can go, too."

Birdsong smiled and turned to look at Suzy.

"I want to go," she nodded.

§

"When a crazy person 'moves on,' are they still crazy?" Fin asked. "Do they take that with them?"

Fin was trying to keep his mind off of the fact that they were hiking through the forest alone in the dark toward where they thought the 7:30 mine trail was. He was using the flashlight app on his phone to light their way, but it was still rather disconcerting.

"I have no idea," Suzy replied. She pondered the question as they continued trudging on through the dark forest, her hands gripping his arm tightly. "I mean, if you believe in reincarnation, I suppose it could account for the occasional baby born with brain damage with no apparent genetic predisposition." Her voice sounded calm, but Fin thought he could detect a slight tenseness to it.

Suzy had been very happy for Birdsong and Honeybee, to finally be able to move on to the next plane after so long. But after the twin flashes of white light, she and Fin realized how alone they were on the mountainside. Suddenly engulfed in near total darkness, Fin had immediately snatched up his phone out of its holster on his belt and turned on the flashlight.

"Are you sure I did the right thing, keeping the spearhead?" he asked

"That's not really for me to say," Suzy replied, thinking seriously about his question. "It's not connected to Birdsong anymore. It could just be considered a relic of an ancient past. At the same time, it's what killed her, and it was lodged in what was left of her body for countless years, maybe centuries, before it ended up where you found it. But the fact that you're not trying to profit off of that, but you're placing it in sort of a place of honor demonstrates the high regard you've given it.

"If you had left it up here on the mountain, who's to say that someone else, with less respect for the people connected to it, or even just its history, wouldn't find it and desecrate it and her memory, knowingly or unknowingly?"

Fin nodded, thinking about his collection.

"You know, it's weird. I collected those arrowheads because I thought they were cool, an interesting bit of local history. I never gave any thought to who or what they might have been connected to back in their day."

"I assume you've never been visited by Native American ghosts."

"No, I haven't." He thought for a few moments. "At least, not that I was aware of before. But with my new-found ghost psychic abilities, who knows what awaits me in the future?"

"So," Suzy said as they continued through the dark forest, "you could understand them, huh?"

"Yeah, it was the weirdest thing! It was like I was suddenly hearing the ghosts speak in English, and they could, apparently, understand me, too."

"Well, like I said a few days ago, the more open you are, the more likely you'll be able make contact." Fin shivered, and Suzy felt it. "What's wrong?" she asked.

"I'm just not sure how much contact I want with ghosts. I have to admit I'm still a little creeped out by them. Especially ghosts like Stone Face."

"Just think how much time we'll save, if you can see the episodes, too. I won't have to spend all that time telling you what I saw. You'll be able to time travel yourself, instead of just living vicariously through me."

"Yeah, I suppose."

"Hey, maybe *you* could go up to that haunted hotel you mentioned and send their ghost away." Fin couldn't see her face, but he could tell, now, by her voice, that she was being a smartass.

They walked several yards in silence before Suzy spoke up.

"This is so creepy!" she said, squeezing his arm. "Talk to me."

Rather than asking for a prompt this time, he said what was on his mind at the moment.

"I wish you didn't have to go back home so soon."

"I know. Just one more day." She was quiet for a few moments. "But we have lots of time."

"If there's anything that these ghost stories teach me," Fin replied, "it's that we don't know how long we have. Melody was only twenty-one."

"You're right." Suzy walked several more steps thinking about Melody, wondering how her transition went.

"One of my favorite movie quotes," Fin said, interrupting her thoughts, "is from *When Harry Met Sally*. Billy Crystal said, 'When you realize you want to spend the rest of your life with somebody, you want the rest of your life to start as soon as possible.'"

"You're always quoting movies," Suzy said. Fin couldn't see her face, but tried to determine her tone of voice. He wasn't sure if she was impressed, or just exasperated, but he thought he knew the answer. "How do you have time to watch all those movies enough times to remember the quotations?"

"Honey, if there's one thing I've learned, it's that you have to *make* time for what's important." He grinned, but his face quickly became serious again.

"Fin, the rest of your life has already started. It's going on now, and we're in it."

"Yeah, but you're leaving the day after tomorrow. And as I already said, anything could happen."

"Then I guess you better get your ass out to Marblehead. It's your turn, now."

Before he could respond to her snarky comment, they noticed the forest thinning ahead, a less intense darkness in front of them. A few moments later, they emerged from the forest and onto the gravel trail.

They both heaved a sigh of relief as they began the trek downward.

After trudging carefully down the long gravel trail in the dark, it was nearly an hour later when they finally reached Fin's car, exhausted and shivering from the dropping temperatures. They opened the doors, but before they could climb in, Fin gasped and turned to Suzy.

"Do you hear that?" he asked.

Suzy stood still and listened, tilting her head. Wafting down the mountainside came a haunting sound. It sounded like distant violin music.

www.ingramcontent.com/pod-product-compliance
Lightning Source LLC
Chambersburg PA
CBHW020408180626
46812CB00003B/884
9781733502252